DROWNING BY NUMBERS

by the same author

A ZED AND TWO NOUGHTS

THE BELLY OF AN ARCHITECT

DROWNING BY NUMBERS

Peter Greenaway

faber and faber
LONDON · BOSTON

First published in 1988
by Faber and Faber Limited
3 Queen Square London WC1N 3AU

Photoset by Wilmaset Birkenhead Wirral
Printed in Great Britain by
Richard Clay Ltd Bungay Suffolk

All rights reserved

© Peter Greenaway, 1988

This book is sold subject to the condition that it shall not, by way of trade or otherwise, be lent, resold, hired out or otherwise circulated without the publisher's prior consent in any form of binding or cover other than that in which it is published and without a similar condition including this condition being imposed on the subsequent purchaser.

British Library Cataloguing in Publication Data

Greenaway, Peter
Drowning by numbers
I. Title
822'.914

ISBN 0–571–15371–2

Contents

Introduction	vii
Drowning by Numbers	1
The Number Count	115

Introduction

The first version of *Drowning by Numbers* was written in 1982 whilst the editing of *The Draughtsman's Contract* was taking place. There have been several versions since then but they have differed very little in plot, game-playing and characterization from the original. The version that follows is the version that everyone worked to during principal photography in Suffolk in the autumn of 1987.

Cissie Colpitts has a longer history still. As a single entity and not three people, she appeared in 1976 as a companion to Tulse Luper in *Vertical Features Remake* and had a biography all to herself in the 1978 version of *The Falls*. Even then she had a wary respect for water-towers, for it was while standing on the top of the water-tower at Goole 'watching the fires at Hull' that she suffered from the effects of the VUE – the Violent Unknown Event. After bleeding from the mouth, she developed vertigo, pernicious anaemia, splayed thumbs and an attraction to the dark of cinemas.

In *Drowning by Numbers* she is three people – grandmother, daughter and grand-daughter – three generations of solidarity taking action against marital dissatisfaction. Tulse Luper, her lover's name in *The Falls*, has perhaps become Henry Madgett – halfway between 'maggot' and 'magic'. Ostensibly a coroner but really a primary game-player, he relieves the tripartite Cissie Colpitts of her criminal responsibilities and gets precious little in return.

But as though in recompense Cissie's ending has already been charted. In some future project, made singular again, as a grand old lady of ninety-two, she quietly passes away in a cinema in Philadelphia, haemorrhaging into a crimson-plush cinema seat while watching Renoir's *Boudu Sauve des Eaux*. She was still interested in drowning.

Peter Greenaway
March 1988

Drowning by Numbers was first screened as part of the Official competition at the Cannes Film Festival on 19 May 1988. The cast included:

CISSIE COLPITTS 1	Joan Plowright
CISSIE COLPITTS 2	Juliet Stevenson
CISSIE COLPITTS 3	Joely Richardson
MADGETT	Bernard Hill
SMUT	Jason Edwards
JAKE	Bryan Pringle
HARDY	Trevor Cooper
BELLAMY	David Morrissey
SKIPPING GIRL	Nathalie Morse
GREGORY	John Rogan
TEIGAN	Paul Mooney
NANCY	Jane Gurnett
JONAH BOGNOR	Kenny Ireland
MOSES BOGNOR	Michael Percival
SID THE DIGGER	Arthur Spreckley
MRS HARDY	Joanna Dickins
MARINA BELLAMY	Janine Duvitski
70 VAN DYKE	Michael Fitzgerald
71 VAN DYKE	Edward Tudor-Pole
HARE	Vanni Corbellini
POLICE CORONER	Ian Talbot
POLICEMAN	Roderick Leigh
Casting Director	Sharon Howard Field
Director of Photography	Sacha Vierny
Camera Operator	Adam Rogers
Art Directors	Ben van Os
	Jan Roelfs
Costumes	Heather Williams
Sound	Garth Marshall
Editor	John Wilson
Assistant Editor	Milfid Ellis
Sound Editor	Chris Wyatt
Music	Michael Nyman
Creative Consultant	Walter Donohue

Producers   Kees Kasander
                         Denis Wigman
Director   Peter Greenaway

An Allarts Production

Photographs by Stephen Morley

Section 1: *Skipping Girl's House*

1. EXT. SKIPPING GIRL'S HOUSE. NIGHT
Start with a star-filled sky that suggests the universe but is idealized like a nocturnal nursery illustration by Maurice Sendak. The accompanying music is loud, cathedral-resonant, and sharply rhythmic; it has an insistent double pulse that will eventually and gradually give precedence to an unexplained double sound – a regular, quick slapping and swishing. Travel slowly and vertically down the star-filled sky to the chimney and roof ridge of a modest row of terraced houses. Slowly introduce a young GIRL's voice counting between the slapping and swishing '. . . 21 . . . Deneb . . . 22 . . . Spica . . . 23 . . . Rigel . . .'
Continue to travel down to reveal the guttering and the rainwater pipes and an open, lighted, second-floor bedroom window. Behind and through the lace curtains, and partly obscured by a vase of blood-red and purple peonies, a man lies naked on top of a woman on a shadowy bed. '. . . 31 . . . Regulus . . . 32 . . . Altair . . . 33 . . . Capella . . .'
Travel on down past the street sign AMSTERDAM ROAD, and the door lintel and the doorway. The GIRL's voice now dominates the soundtrack . . . and the GIRL is revealed . . . a dim, orange light behind her down a corridor lined with floral wallpaper. The rope is slapping the door jamb every time it passes over her head. She is wearing a white dress with dark stars on it (the reverse of the night sky) decorated with elaborate bows – she looks set for a children's party. The skipping rope is white with japanned red handles '. . . 42 . . . Vega . . . 43 . . . Sirius . . . 44 . . . Nekkor . . .' The GIRL is pale and could have escaped from Velázquez's *Las Meninas* . . . she looks unreal . . . her expression is much too old or too knowing for her age.
The camera, after watching the GIRL skip for '. . . 45 . . . Eridani . . . 46 . . . Canopus . . . 47 . . . Arcturus . . .', begins to track slowly backwards out across the road – the SKIPPING GIRL held exactly in the middle of frame – '. . . 51 . . . Antares . . . 52 . . . Betelgeuse . . . 53 . . . Fomalhaut . . .' – and red letters spell out the primary credits discreetly along the lower

frame. '... 67 ... Pulcherima ... 68 ... Algarab ... 69 ... Bellatrix ...'
The slow track back ends across the road where a shallow puddle reflects the terraced row of houses and the stars in the deep ultramarine sky. Superimpose the title: DROWNING BY NUMBERS.
Beside the puddle, stuck in the mud, is a stake sloppily painted or sprayed with chrome yellow paint ... some of the paint has spattered on the ashy ground roundabout.

2. EXT. SKIPPING GIRL'S HOUSE. NIGHT

Sharp cut to two looming figures, walking down the darkly lit street. A street light is behind them, haloing the hairs on their heads, making a dark space of their features, throwing their shadows towards the camera. One is a large woman – NANCY, a gauche seamstress, big-boned and plain. She is a shop assistant aged twenty-three, unused to drinking and now worse for it. Despite advanced tipsiness, which is shot through with nervousness as well as drink, she has a good voice. She is singing:

>   NANCY: . . . seven in the bed,
>   and the little one said,
>   Roll over, roll over.
>   And they all rolled over
>   And one fell out,
>   And bumped his head,
>   And shouted out,
>   Please remember that single beds
>   Are only meant for 1 2 3 4 5 6 7
>   in the bed
>   And the little one said . . .

She is also dancing – a jerky waltz step – around her partner. She dances like a peasant in a Brueghel painting – long skirts, heavy, uncomfortable shoes, a leather belt and a big nose.

Her partner has the same heaviness. He is the gardener, JAKE, the husband of CISSIE COLPITTS 1. He is in his mid-sixties, with a muscular body and a full beard that catches the back light. He looks like a hermit by Velázquez; in fact they both look somewhat biblical – like Joseph and Mary with the age difference very noticeable.

To JAKE, NANCY is easy game. He is used to drink, infidelity and general gross behaviour. As NANCY comes to the end of each count, he grabs at her breast or lunges at her thighs, and at the line '. . . and the little one said . . .' he makes obscene gestures with his finger and NANCY giggles and dances clumsily away.

The two drunks amble by, NANCY giddily dancing. They take no notice of the SKIPPING GIRL, nor she of them . . . 'Mirach . . . 89 Regulus . . . 90 Crucis . . . 91 . . .'

3. EXT. SKIPPING GIRL'S HOUSE. NIGHT
Another figure approaches. She walks slowly, growing steadily larger.
The woman on the dark street, her hair backlit by a street lamp, is CISSIE COLPITTS 1, the wife of JAKE the gardener. CISSIE COLPITTS 1 is a grandmother, aged sixty-eight. She wears a dark print dress, discreetly patterned with small flowers. She is unmistakably a grandmother and bound to smell of clean linen and lavender, with an apple in her pocket. She walks unhesitatingly towards the flashing rope.

GIRL: . . . 98 . . . Procyon . . . 99 . . . Aldebaran . . . 100 . . . Electra.
(*The* GIRL *stops skipping and counting. The silence that follows is heavy. Very quietly* CISSIE COLPITTS 1 *speaks.*)
CISSIE 1: What are you doing up so late?
GIRL: I'm counting the stars.
CISSIE 1: Do you really know all their names?
GIRL: Yes I do.
(*There is a long pause.*)
CISSIE 1: How many did you count?
GIRL: A hundred.
CISSIE 1: But there are more than a hundred.
GIRL: I know.
(*There is a longer pause in complete silence.*)
CISSIE 1: Why did you stop?
GIRL: A hundred is enough. Once you have counted one hundred, all other hundreds are the same.
(*They both stand quietly, self-absorbed.*)

Section 2: *The House of Cissie Colpitts 1*

4. EXT. HOUSE OF CISSIE COLPITTS 1 – FRONT DOOR. NIGHT
NUMBER 1 – the first number in the series 1–100 – appears on a front door of a cottage. The door has been much overpainted and is overhung with honeysuckle.
It's three o'clock in the morning and up against the door, the gardener JAKE roughly fumbles the seamstress NANCY who has her head thrown back and is trying to drink from a bottle. JAKE is at her throat, working his way to her breasts. The door flies open and inwards and bangs violently against the inside wall.

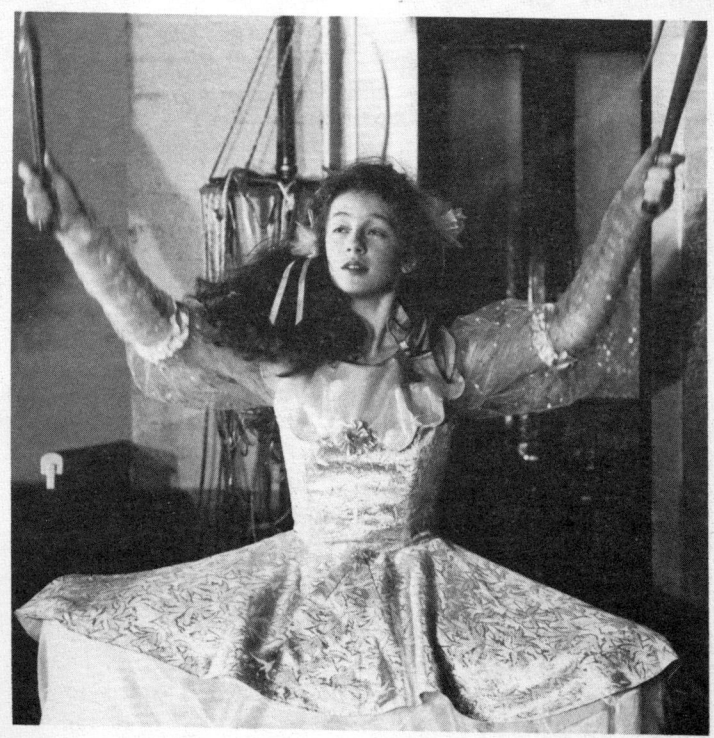

5. INT. THE HOUSE OF CISSIE COLPITTS I – KITCHEN.
NIGHT
The drunken pair (JAKE and NANCY) fall in. There is convulsed struggling and a sudden sharp scream and then laughing. They have fallen into a dimly lit kitchen.
>NANCY: Even for a gardener you smell. Are you afraid of water?
>JAKE: I'll wash and you can wash with me.
>NANCY: I'm clean enough.
>JAKE: We'll see . . . let me smell . . .
>NANCY: Get your nose out of there.
>JAKE: You could do with a bath, girl . . . you smell of shops . . . what do you wipe yourself with, brown paper? Cissie's got some pink soap.
>NANCY: Leave Cissie out of it.
>(JAKE *shakily gets up and switches on a light. He picks up a pink bar of soap and throws it to* NANCY – *she adroitly catches it.*)
>JAKE: You're not a bad catch – for a woman.

6. EXT. THE HOUSE OF CISSIE COLPITTS I – FIELD. NIGHT
The dark silhouette of cows, some standing, some sitting on a hard grass incline against a starry sky. From nowhere CISSIE I silently appears among them, walking across damp grass. The cows do not move and are not perturbed.
Her point of view sees a view of moonlit fields, a star-filled sky, cows and a moonlit track leading to a view of a solitary house with a single light on.

7. INT. THE HOUSE OF CISSIE COLPITTS I – KITCHEN.
NIGHT
From floor level, a stream of hot steaming water arcs in backlit artificial light into a resonant tin tub. There is a glimpse of a copper pan, a white enamel jug, dark-red flagstones and NANCY sitting on the floor, her feet towards the camera – the soles naked and dirty. She bends forward to scratch her leg, and sits inelegantly – the camera can suggestively see up her thick, brown-coloured skirt.
Taking buckets of hot water off a gas stove, JAKE pours more hot water into the bath.
>JAKE: Get your clothes off, girl.
>NANCY: (*From the floor*) My name's Nellie and there's not room in that bath for two of us.

JAKE: Who says two's going in it?
NANCY: I'm surprised you haven't got a proper bathroom.
JAKE: I like a tin bath.
(JAKE *brings a table lamp nearer. It has a trailing flex of frayed red. He bends down and places it on the floor deliberately to light up her legs under her skirt.* NANCY *moves to stop him.*)
NANCY: Take that light further off.
JAKE: What are you frightened of? Are you ashamed of me seeing your underwear – or aren't you wearing any?
NANCY kneels, looking at her reflection in the water in the bath. JAKE kneels with her and attempts to put his hand up her skirt. A large vase of anemones goes over, flooding the tiles. They slither in the spilt water and crush the flowers.
In spilt water, spilt milk and a clatter of pans, clothes get taken off and fall on the wet floor. Between drinks from the same bottle, details of clothing, hair and flesh get revealed – thick brown plaits, a large dimpled knee, a nipple, fumbling fingers. On more than one occasion JAKE instinctively smooths down his moustache. Taking off his shirt – it reveals – on the collar – a laundry mark – NUMBER 2 in the film series. Piles of neatly folded, newly laundered linen and underwear get knocked to the floor.
A delicate white china cup full of lemon slices gets knocked off a table, smashes and cuts NANCY's foot. She screams and winces. She stands and balances on one leg. JAKE, on his knees, licks the blood from a cut, drags his tongue up her leg to her thigh, lifts her slip and pulls down her pants.
NANCY: I'm cold standing here. I want a bath too.
JAKE: There's one on the wall outside.
(NANCY *splashes into one side of the tub and out the other.* JAKE *grabs at her, whips off her slip and slaps her backside.*)
Moonlight's good for the complexion.

8. EXT. THE HOUSE OF CISSIE COLPITTS I – BACK GARDEN. NIGHT
The back of the house, illuminated in the moonlight. There is indeed a tin bath hanging on the outside wall. The house is surrounded by a lush, dark, well-kept garden – thick clumps of mallow, sweetpeas, lupins and evening primrose covered in nocturnal moths.
A bonfire quietly and unobtrusively smokes in a corner. The white/grey smoke spiralling up in the dark – the slightest

suggestion of red sparks. It is a moment or two before CISSIE COLPITTS I is seen standing there, just outside a neat, white-painted gate – her features partly hidden in flower shadow.

9. EXT. THE HOUSE OF CISSIE COLPITTS I – BACK GARDEN. NIGHT
The kitchen door throws a strip of yellow light across the garden. The door opens and a naked and hopping NANCY comes out, locates the bath and struggles with it in order to lift it off the wall. She and the bath collapse into a flowerbed with a clatter and a scream.

10. EXT. THE HOUSE OF CISSIE COLPITTS I – BACK GARDEN. NIGHT
Seen from inside the house, the two figures struggle to drag the bath through the door. JAKE is dark brown and NANCY is very white – contrasting like Adam and Eve in a Van Eyck painting. They are both absurd, and for a moment, innocent, against the background of the night. Moths and beetles fly in the door attracted by the bright light.

11. INT. THE HOUSE OF CISSIE COLPITTS I – KITCHEN. NIGHT
Fluttering moths and light-dazed beetles skitter about on the red tiles of the floor, casting large agitated shadows.

12. EXT. THE HOUSE OF CISSIE COLPITTS I – BACK GARDEN. NIGHT
There is a silence in the garden with a slight breeze. CISSIE I has picked a bunch of flowers, and she slowly shreds the leaves from a stem.

13. INT. THE HOUSE OF CISSIE COLPITTS I – KITCHEN. NIGHT
JAKE and NANCY are copulating on the floor. There are nettle blisters on NANCY's thighs and a burnet moth walks across JAKE's back.

14. EXT. THE HOUSE OF CISSIE COLPITTS I – BACK GARDEN. NIGHT
CISSIE's face is at the window – the panes are clustered with fluttering insects attracted to the light.
She turns away and stares absently down the garden.

15. INT. THE HOUSE OF CISSIE COLPITTS I – KITCHEN.
NIGHT

JAKE and NANCY are lying in two tubs of steaming water. The tubs are symmetrical and facing the camera like a respectable double bed of water. JAKE drinks from the bottle, she soaps her hands with pink soap – the soap by far the most colourful object in the frame. They look like a married couple in bed. The neat kitchen is seen to be in disarray. Pans, flowers, towels, clothes, underwear litter the floor. On the wall above and behind the two baths is a large *Nurseryman's Calendar*. The camera makes a point of noticing it. It is dated the 3rd in bright-red letters and numerals (NUMBER 3). Above the numeral is a brightly coloured photograph of red flowers – set out as a flower-growers' catalogue – all shades of red – scarlet poppies, dark-red anemones, crimson dahlias, red roses . . . Underneath the calendar – hanging in pride of place – is a garden fork, its prongs extravagantly polished, shining in the artificial light. It is a prize fork with an inscription on the metal shaft.

Into the kitchen, CISSIE COLPITTS I makes a grand entrance – slightly sinister – blossoms fall on to the floor. She looks like Ceres or Mother Earth, leaves and flowers are stuck to her dress. She is surrounded by fluttering insects that have come in with her, attracted to the light. Her entrance is dramatically lit from below – from the light on the floor. She looks beautiful and more desirable than the snoring woman in the bath.

CISSIE I sits down on an open-work kitchen chair and carefully puts her bunch of lupins and peonies in a large canister on the floor; beyond her, JAKE starts, tries to sit up but ineffectually flops about in the water.

JAKE: Cissie – ah – we've been using your soap. Nancy smells like a baby – don't you, girl?
NANCY: My name is Nellie.
(*There is no reply from* CISSIE *who sits and watches them.*)
JAKE: It's her birthday today. I took her out to celebrate. Why don't you wish her happy birthday, Cissie? Look – she's as naked as the day she was born . . . nothing wrong in that, is there, Cissie? . . . *You're* not supposed to be here at all. You're supposed to be out playing cards – backgammon, Newmarket, whist, two-in-a-row, three-in-a-bed, four-in-hand [NUMBER 4] . . . along with your friend Madgett . . .

(NANCY *convulses and vomits. Instinctively, she vomits outside of the bath.*)
Get her a towel, Cissie – she's drunken too much.
(NANCY *falls asleep.* JAKE *makes a feeble movement and fails to get out of the bath – he is far too drunk to take any calculated action.*)
If you play your cards right here, Cissie, we'll let you take your clothes off and you can get in too.
(CISSIE I *gets up from her chair and without much effort pushes* JAKE *under the water with the flat of her hand. Blossoms from her dress fall in the water. He struggles. She counts 'one' under her breath. She lets him go.*)
I don't need a wash, Cissie. I've had one. Nancy did it for me.
(*He sounds sad and resigned.* CISSIE I *pushes him under again. She counts 'two'. He struggles, spluttering.*)
Nancy did it for me. How about a game of . . .
CISSIE I pushes him under again. She counts 'three'. Bubbles froth up. CISSIE I calmly pulls strands of hair off her face with one hand and drowns him with the other. She releases him and he slowly rises.
CISSIE I kneels and listens to his heart, her hair on the water line. She looks at him . . . weeps . . . kisses his forehead, and smooths down his moustache in a way reminiscent of the way he would do it himself. NANCY snores.

16. INT. THE HOUSE OF CISSIE COLPITTS I – KITCHEN. DAWN
A very early dawn begins to break at the window; CISSIE I switches off the light and turns off the gas taps – the gas mark on the oven is 5 (NUMBER 5). She takes JAKE's favourite garden fork from the wall under the calendar and fingers its long glinting prongs.

17. EXT. THE HOUSE OF CISSIE COLPITTS I – BACK GARDEN. DAWN
Carrying the fork outside, CISSIE I throws it on the bonfire – treading the wooden shaft into the glow of smouldering twigs – a few sparks fly up against the dawn sky, illuminating her dress, face and hair.

18. INT. THE HOUSE OF CISSIE COLPITTS I – KITCHEN.
DAWN
Going inside as the first cock cries, CISSIE picks up the phone by the front door and dials a number (NUMBER 6). The bonfire dimly illuminates the bodies lying in the bath tubs – through the open door a dull pink glows on their white flesh.

Section 3: Madgett's House

19. EXT. MADGETT'S HOUSE – BEACH. DAWN
An isolated house beside a wide tidal river with a beach. The front door of the house is open on to the foreshore and throws a swathe of warm light on to sheep – some thirty or forty animals – milling and bleating in a front garden. They are impatiently waiting to be let out through a gate in a hedge on to the beach. A large man – MADGETT – with a coat pulled over pyjamas, and a thin wiry man in his sixties – GREGORY – dressed like a fisherman, are letting them out. The warm yellow light from the house glimmers in the eyes of the sheep and is absorbed by their dirty fleeces. The phone in the house rings unanswered.

20. INT. MADGETT'S HOUSE – SMUT'S BEDROOM. DAWN
Upstairs in the same house – with the considerable noise of the sheep heard in the background and the ringing of the phone heard at a different distance – is a dark, crowded bedroom. Around a large double bed are desks, tables and chairs, bedside lamps and trestles piled high with miscellaneous objects – prominent among them are collections of photographic equipment – cameras, lenses, discarded film boxes – 'philosophical toys' – objects like praxinoscopes, magic lanterns. There are maps and diagrams, games of ludo – and directly beside the bed, on a table, is balanced a playing-card castle made up entirely of cards of the seven of hearts (NUMBER 7). In the dark (barely lit by the dawn light through the uncurtained windows) a boy, aged around ten, stirs in the middle of the large double bed. His name is SMUT. He is MADGETT's son. The noise of the sheep and the ringing of the phone have awakened him. He stretches and searches the bedside table for a light switch. He finds it, switches it on and a table lamp illuminates his face and the pillow. He blinks and reaches for his spectacles. He puts them on. As he sits in the bed, blinking,

the phone stops ringing at the selfsame instant as the pack-of-cards castle collapses without observable reason. SMUT closes his eyes.

Dawn Card Castles
  SMUT: (*Voice over*) In the game of Dawn Card Castles, fifty-two playing-cards are stacked up into a castle in a draught-free space: the player can determine the dreams of the next night if he awakes before the castle collapses. Those players who wish to dream of Romance build their castles with the seven of hearts.

Section 4: The House of Cissie Colpitts 2

21. EXT. HOUSE OF CISSIE COLPITTS 2 – EARLY MORNING
The morning has advanced – it's brighter. CISSIE 1 wheels her bike across a gravelled drive towards a house beside the sea.

22. EXT. HOUSE OF CISSIE COLPITTS 2 – WINDOW. EARLY MORNING
Through a frame of early-morning sky the sun comes up behind dramatic clouds. A scattering of small stones arc and clatter on glass, then bounce down out of sight.
A second scatter of small stones clatters on the glass and disappears.

23. INT. HOUSE OF CISSIE COLPITTS 2 – BEDROOM. EARLY MORNING
A bedroom interior looking towards the window. The sun is beginning to shine dramatically into the room, and on to a double bed, very white-sheeted, with a man and a woman in bed. The woman sits up – she is naked with her back to camera. Beside the bed is a digital alarm clock indicating eight o'clock (NUMBER 8).
As she treads across the bed to get to the window she pulls the white sheet off her naked sleeping husband. He is fat. His name is HARDY.

24. INT. HOUSE OF CISSIE COLPITTS 2 – BEDROOM. EARLY MORNING
The sun reflects blindingly on the pane. The woman in the double bed peers out. The sun blinds her, she covers her breasts with her forearm. The woman is CISSIE COLPITTS 2. The elder CISSIE's daughter. She is thirty-two. Her body is always, summer and winter, sun-tanned.
    CISSIE 2: Who's out there, for God's sake?
    CISSIE 1: It's me – get up, I want to tell you something.
    CISSIE 2: Mother, it had better be good.
(*She relaxes and takes her arm away from her breasts.*)

25. EXT. HOUSE OF CISSIE COLPITTS 2 – FRONT. EARLY MORNING
The front of the house. All four windows – two up and two down – are blazing with the reflected light of the rising sun. CISSIE 1, the grandmother, stands symmetrically between the bottom two windows. She treads the gravel, not looking up.
    CISSIE 1: It's Jake.
    CISSIE 2: (*In a stagy whisper*) What?
    CISSIE 1: Jake has drunk too much again.

26. INT. HOUSE OF CISSIE COLPITTS 2 – BEDROOM. EARLY MORNING
Inside the bedroom, with only moderate haste, CISSIE 2, the daughter, quietly dresses herself; she carefully puts a scarlet beret on her head before any other clothes. She moves back and forth, in and out of the blaze of bright light coming in through the window. After an interval – a surprisingly short interval – CISSIE 1, the grandmother, comes quietly through the bedroom

door. The man (HARDY) in the bed stirs and, completely asleep, naturally rearranges himself in a laid-out-corpse position with his mouth open and the sheet around his ankles.

CISSIE 1: (*Staring at her son-in-law*) He's put a lot of weight on recently.
CISSIE 2: Mother, ssh. You'll wake him and he'll want to eat. The only time he stops eating is when he's asleep. (*Offering dress*) Is it warm enough for this dress?
CISSIE 1: Yes – I've phoned Madgett – he doesn't answer.
CISSIE 2: What did you want to do that for?
CISSIE 1: I've just drowned Jake . . . (*Looking at her son-in-law*) Do all fat men have little penises?
CISSIE 2: I don't know, Mother – I've not known . . . what do you mean?
CISSIE 1: When you first met Hardy did he have a moustache?
CISSIE 2: What do you mean, you just drowned Jake?
CISSIE 1: I don't like the beard.
CISSIE 2: Neither do I. I'm trying to persuade him to shave it off. What do you mean, you've just drowned Jake?
CISSIE 1: Yes, I need your help to move her.
CISSIE 2: You what? Move who?
CISSIE 1: Nancy.
CISSIE 2: Nancy who?

CISSIE 1: Nancy Gill, she calls herself Nell, but everyone . . .
CISSIE 2: What's she got to do with it? God, have you drowned her too?
CISSIE 1: He doesn't smell very fresh does he? . . . He looks pregnant. I like these creases here.
(*She touches* HARDY's *stomach and he stirs.*)
CISSIE 2: Mother! (*She is nearly dressed.*) Are you drunk?
CISSIE 1: No . . . just very, very sad.
(*She weeps, hangs her head, her hands in her lap.*)
CISSIE 2: Come downstairs.
CISSIE 1: (*At the door – and said with sudden brightness*) Oh, I must get rid of these. (*She empties a pocketful of gravel on the dressing-table.*) It's your gravel.
(*On the dressing-table is a key-ring with a number 9 motif* (NUMBER 9).)
CISSIE 2: Well, thank you, Mother, you might have emptied it outside where it belongs.
CISSIE 1: Well – you know – Virginia Woolf.
CISSIE 2: What?
CISSIE 1: We had better try Madgett again.
(*She picks up the phone from the landing table and hands it to her daughter.*)
He can probably help us.
CISSIE 2: Us, Mother? – God, it sounds as though you might be serious.
(*She dials a number – the same number as before.*)

Section 5: Madgett's House

27. INT. MADGETT'S HOUSE – HALL/STAIRWAY. EARLY MORNING

SMUT's defenestration exercises. In Madgett's house beside the river the phone is ringing distantly.
SMUT, wearing his pyjama trousers, is standing in the hallway with the front door open on to the garden and the river behind him. He takes off his spectacles, puts them away in a crush-proof box tied with a string around his neck. He sways on his feet and, facing a long carpeted stairway going up to an open window, he counts to ten in a low voice (NUMBER 10) and rushes, clumping, up the stairs and hurls himself out of the window in a spectacular dive.

28. EXT. MADGETT'S HOUSE – GARDEN. EARLY MORNING
Cut to SMUT sailing through the air outside and landing on a pile of cardboard boxes and mattresses on the lawn in a sunlit garden. Sitting among the garbage, he myopically searches for his glasses case, takes out his spectacles, puts them on, climbs out from the boxes, walks over to the camera, resets the flash and walks back to the front of the house.
Over this game is a voice-over read carefully by SMUT, describing the game.

Flights of Fancy
> SMUT: (*Voice over*) The game Flights of Fancy or Reverse-Strip-Jump is played from as high a jumping-point as a competitor will dare. After each successful jump, the competitor is allowed to put on an article of clothing. Thirteen jumps is normally more than enough to see a competitor fully dressed for the day.

29. INT. MADGETT'S HOUSE – HALL/STAIRWAY. EARLY MORNING
SMUT enters the house, ticks off the number 11 written on a list tacked to the wall with a drawing pin and writes the number 12 under it with a stub of pencil hanging from the list on a string (NUMBERS 11 and 12). The phone is still ringing. SMUT puts on his shirt and prepares for another jump. He rushes up the stairs.

30. EXT. MADGETT'S HOUSE – GARDEN. EARLY MORNING
Seen from the outside, SMUT comes flying through the window in a dive worthy of a swimming pool. He belly-flops on to the cardboard boxes. The camera flashes, he puts his glasses on for the next go and walks back to the front of the house.
He changes his pyjamas for a pair of short trousers.

31. EXT. MADGETT'S HOUSE – SIDE. EARLY MORNING
TEIGAN – a gaunt, thin young man in glasses – wheels a bike round the side of the house and leans it on the boxes so that the pedals and handlebars stick out menacingly.

32. INT. MADGETT'S HOUSE – HALL/STAIRWAY. EARLY MORNING
SMUT, inside, writes the number 13 after crossing out 12 (NUMBER 13) and rushes upstairs.

33. EXT. MADGETT'S HOUSE – GARDEN. EARLY MORNING
From outside we wait for the flying leap with awful anticipation. It never comes.

34. INT. MADGETT'S HOUSE – SITTING ROOM. EARLY MORNING
The interior of the Madgett sitting room or study.
The room is seen from beside the ringing telephone. It is crowded with furniture and objects. Tables, heavily stuffed armchairs, thick books, paper-crammed files, card indexes and scientific toys; gyroscopes, astrolabes, sextants, stethoscopes, surgical instruments. Cricket bats. The room and its objects are lit with natural light from the right-hand side. The door to the room flies open and lets in bright sunlight from the left-hand side which momentarily animates all the room's objects and furniture. SMUT rushes in and crosses the room to reach for the phone, which, just before he picks it up, stops ringing. He curses. A cock crows – the second cockcrow of the morning. Right beside the telephone and dislodged by SMUT's rush to pick up the phone, are a number of stencils – some of them heavily marked with red and yellow paint – they fall in a cascade – numbers 11, 12, 13, 14 and 15 (NUMBERS 14 and 15).

Section 6: *The House of Cissie Colpitts 1*

35. EXT. HOUSE OF CISSIE COLPITTS 1 – FRONT. DAY
The rising sun is warming the walls.
Round the corner of the house comes the daughter, CISSIE COLPITTS 2. She is pushing a large wooden wheelbarrow. After her comes her mother – CISSIE COLPITTS 1. CISSIE 1 is carrying a large eiderdown, which is put into the barrow and plumped up.
The two women go back into the house and struggle out through the door with the wet, heavy, white, naked body of NANCY – she is still completely comatose with the effects of drinking.
The women go back into the house for a third time while NANCY's sleeping body lies in the barrow among the flowers and butterflies of CISSIE 1's cottage garden.

36. EXT. HOUSE OF CISSIE COLPITTS 1 – FRONT. DAY
The two CISSIES come out of the house. CISSIE 1 is carrying a basket of mushrooms, CISSIE 2, Nancy's copious clothing. CISSIE 1 shuts and locks the house door.

    CISSIE 2: Look at all these – it must have taken ages to undress. This is nice . . .
    (*She tries a decorated undergarment up against herself.*)

CISSIE 1, after putting the basket of mushrooms beside NANCY in the barrow, goes over to the smouldering bonfire. With her foot and a stick, she pulls out JAKE's garden fork which she threw into the fire earlier. The wooden shaft is virtually burnt away and the blackened prongs still look vicious.

    CISSIE 1: Jake never let me use this fork.
    CISSIE 2: Now he's not here to stop you – except that you've now ruined it.
    CISSIE 1: There were times when this fork gave him more satisfaction than I did.
    (CISSIE 2 *giggles and* CISSIE 1 *throws the fork down back into the fire.*)
    Although it's surprising for a gardener to say it – he always wanted to be cremated – he said you're not permitted to grow rhubarb in a cemetery . . . so why bury your body there and waste your fertilizer . . .

The two women wheel the barrow through an orchard. For the first time we can see the other side of the barrow – there is number 16 (NUMBER 16) burnt into the side.

37. EXT. ORCHARD. DAY
    CISSIE 1: Doesn't she look white? Poor girl. Needs some sun.
    CISSIE 2: What are you going to say if we meet someone?
    CISSIE 1: Depends who it is. 'Morning, (*She giggles.*) just taking Nancy home – she's been sleeping with my husband.' . . . I suppose you can see why Jake fancied her.
    CISSIE 2: Cover her up.
    CISSIE 1: Why?
    CISSIE 2: She could lose some weight.
    CISSIE 1: Everyone seems to be getting fatter. Jake must have thought that things were getting better all the time. When your father died I was thirty-five. And plump enough. Look at her thumbs – seamstress's thumbs – well turned.
    CISSIE 2: Was Jake interested in thumbs?

CISSIE 1: (*With a laugh*) Not especially, as I remember.
CISSIE 2: What's that?

38. EXT. HEDGE. DAY
They both freeze, having heard a noise the other side of a hedge. They stand still – two women dappled in sun and shadow, and a naked woman in a barrow.
On the other side of the hedge a man walks across the grass carrying a shiny well-polished spade over his shoulder. The man is SID – an odd-jobbing gardener who is never separated from his spade. He is a gaunt man. He wears boots and an ancient trilby hat.
As the CISSIES wait for the man to pass, CISSIE 1 begins to twitch her nose, sniffing at something.
   CISSIE 2: Mother – are you going to sneeze?
   (*She puts her hand up to smother the noise.*)
   CISSIE 1: No – I can smell something.
In the hedge among rich vegetation is a red-painted post. Red paint has been sprayed around it – over the leaves and flowers. On a patch of trodden ground beside it is a red-painted, stencilled number – number 17 (NUMBER 17). Around the number and the post is a scattering of feathers. CISSIE 2 bends down to look.
   CISSIE 2: It's Smut . . .
   CISSIE 1: Madgett must keep him from using that paint – he makes such a mess. What's the smell?
   CISSIE 2: Gunpowder. Smut's been celebrating a corpse.
   (*She bends down and touches the red-painted post – the paint comes off on her fingers.*)
   It's still wet!
The mention of a corpse triggers CISSIE 1 into tears. CISSIE 2 goes to comfort her but stops, waving her red-painted fingers in the air, not wishing to smudge paint on her mother's dress.

Section 7: *Nancy's House*

39. EXT. NANCY'S HOUSE – FRONT GARDEN. DAY
The women wheel the barrow up the front path, alongside a collection of rabbit hutches which are numbered 17, 18, 19, 20 and 21 – the numbers worn, scuffed, partly illegible (NUMBERS 17, 18, 19, 20, 21). Along the front hedge of NANCY's garden

and caught up in the branches of the hedge are strands of brightly coloured paper – the lure thrown out by the 'hare' – the front runner in a game of cross-country paperchase.

40. INT. NANCY'S HOUSE – BEDROOM. DAY
The two women enter NANCY's bedroom, stumble over many pairs of shoes and gladly let NANCY's body down on to the bed. NANCY plumps down deep in the springy feather bed. CISSIE 2's red-painted fingers have left smudges of red paint on NANCY's leg.
> CISSIE 1: (*Looking at all the shoes*) She did a lot of walking.
> CISSIE 2: What do you mean, 'did' . . . this is the live one.
> CISSIE 1: She's got good feet. What's she reading?
> (CISSIE 1 *picks up a paperback of* Catch 22 *from a group of paperbacks beside the bed* (NUMBER 22). *She sits down on the edge of the bed and starts to read.*)
> CISSIE 2: I don't think somehow that she slept in the nude. A nightgown – do you think? And how did she do her hair at night, do you suppose?
> CISSIE 1: You're using 'did' now. Death is catching.
> CISSIE 2: I'm going to phone Madgett again. Third time lucky.

Leaving her mother in the bedroom, the daughter exits, stumbling again over the shoes. On the mantelpiece in the bedroom are a row of birthday cards – some of them marked with Nancy's age – 23 (NUMBER 23).
A cock crows.

Section 8: *Madgett's House*

41. EXT. MADGETT'S HOUSE – BEACH. DAY
Breakfast for four laid on a wooden table on a strip of patchy grass in front of MADGETT's house overlooking the river foreshore. It is still early morning.
MADGETT's garden is crowded with sheep.
Sheep and Tides
> SMUT: (*Voice over*) Sheep are especially sensitive to the exact moment of the turn of the tide. In this game, nine tethered sheep react, pull on the stakes, jolt the chairs and rattle the tea-cups. Bets are taken on the combined sensitivity of any line of three sheep – read vertically, horizontally or

diagonally. Since there are normally three tide-turns every twenty-four hours, it is normal practice to take the best of three results. Reliable clocks, calendars and time-tables are used to determine the accuracy of the sheep's forecast.

CISSIE 2: Madgett, why the hell do you keep all these sheep?

MADGETT: Don't you like them? Shoo them away if you don't like them.

SMUT: (*Approaching* CISSIE 2) Cissie – did you remember?

CISSIE 2: Yes – they're slightly damaged – be careful. Why didn't you answer the phone earlier, Smut?

(CISSIE 2 *takes four fireworks – rockets – from her handbag.* SMUT *puts them in his pocket.*)

SMUT: I never answer the phone till the cock crows three times.

CISSIE 2: Strange boy!

SMUT serves out the last of the breakfast food from a large frying pan. Everywhere he walks he is accompanied by a dog with curlers, its fur caught up in sections of wrapped hair.

Out on the beach, GREGORY and TEIGAN are driving 6-foot-long stakes into the shore sand, and tethering sheep to them with long ropes. Beside each stake is an upright wooden dining chair.

MADGETT: It's nice to see you both so early. How's Hardy?

CISSIE 2: He's all right. (*Pointing at the beach.*) What are they doing?

MADGETT: They're playing Sheep and Tides. Sheep are much maligned, don't you think? Smut and I are testing their intelligence. It's an Old Testament game.

SMUT: No, it's not.

MADGETT: Isn't it? (*Offering* CISSIE 1 *an anonymous cooked organ on the end of his fork*) Have some heart. How's Jake?

CISSIE 1: No, thank you, and Jake's all right.

CISSIE 2: Mother – that's not true.

CISSIE 1: (*Changing the subject and talking to* SMUT, *who has sat down on the grass with a pencil and a thumbed notepad, and is counting the hairs on his dog.*) Smut, what are you doing?

SMUT: 24, 25, 26, 27 . . . I'm just counting the hairs on a dog [NUMBERS 24, 25, 26, 27].

CISSIE 1: Whatever for?

SMUT: To see how many there are.

CISSIE 2: (*Looking directly at* MADGETT) I think you ought to come and see Jake.

(MADGETT *looks up quickly and all three adults exchange significant glances.*)
MADGETT: (*To* SMUT – *it will be noticed that every time* MADGETT *needs to get rid of* SMUT *for a few minutes, he asks him to make tea*) Smut, go and give Gregory and Teigan some tea.
CISSIE 1: What about the sheep?
(SMUT *leaves for the kitchen.*)
MADGETT: They need to be thirsty to be useful. (*Without pausing for breath*) Why do I have to come and see Jake? (*The women don't answer but look down at their plates.*) Is he dead?
CISSIE 1: Good lord, how did you know?
MADGETT: I didn't.
(*There is a pause,* MADGETT *holds his stomach and groans.*) I feel ill.
SMUT: (*Walking past carrying a tray down to the beach*) It's those mushrooms.
MADGETT: I've got to lie down.
(*He gets up from the table.*)
CISSIE 2: For God's sake, Madgett, why have you got to feel ill now? (*To her mother*) I'm going to phone Cissie and tell her that Nancy needs a visit.
(*She leaves the table ahead of* MADGETT.)
CISSIE 1: Madgett, I've got to talk to you about Jake.
MADGETT: Cissie, I can't talk now – I'm ill. Tell Smut when he comes back I need some warm milk with some lemon juice . . . and a straw.
(MADGETT *leaves and* CISSIE 1 *is left alone staring at the river.*)

42. EXT. MADGETT'S HOUSE – BEACH. DAY
SMUT: (*Voice over*) In the game of Sheep and Tides, a referee should be appointed to determine fairplay, distinguishing correct reactions from other interferences. On account of their special relationship with sheep, shepherds are disqualified.
SMUT arrives at the beach where GREGORY and TEIGAN are now playing Sheep and Tides at the water's edge. SMUT puts the tea down on a chair.
TEIGAN: The tide's on the turn now!
GREGORY: No . . . not yet.
TEIGAN: One . . . two . . . three . . . Now!
GREGORY: No, you fool.

TEIGAN: You've missed it.
(*He looks at his watch.*)
GREGORY: You can't go by the book. You have to watch . . . very carefully.

They both peer very intently at the tide. SMUT is returning up the foreshore.

Section 9: Madgett's House

43. INT. MADGETT'S HOUSE – MADGETT'S BEDROOM. DAY
MADGETT is lying down in his bed, with the sheet drawn up to his chin. He lies like a corpse.

CISSIE 1: Can I come in?
MADGETT: Provided you're very considerate.

CISSIE 1 enters the room and sits down beside the bed. MADGETT pulls the sheet up over his head and groans. On the wall above his bed is a large reproduction of Brueghel's painting *Children's Games*.

CISSIE 1: Why do you eat mushrooms?
MADGETT: They're good for coroners. Reminds him of his profession.
CISSIE 1: (*After a pause*) Shall I bring a bowl or a bedpan?
MADGETT: Neither.
CISSIE 1: Madgett, (*Admonishingly*) as you're a coroner . . .
MADGETT: Only to strangers.
CISSIE 1: Treat me as a stranger.
MADGETT: Cissie (*Whipping the sheet off his face*), how can I do that?
CISSIE 1: And you can stop turning everything into a game.
MADGETT: Since when has dying been a game?
CISSIE 2: (*Coming in the door*) Since you became a coroner perhaps?
CISSIE 1: (*Exasperated*) Let him play – it helps his insecurity.
MADGETT: How can I be secure with you around? (*He hides under the sheet again.*) How did he die?
CISSIE 2: He drowned.
MADGETT: (*Coming out from the sheet*) He drowned?
CISSIE 1: In a bath.
MADGETT: (*Back under the sheet*) Is that likely?
CISSIE 2: Of course.
CISSIE 1: He was drunk.

MADGETT: Was he alone?
CISSIE 1: (*After exchanging a conspiratorial look with her daughter*) Of course.
MADGETT: Cissie, are you telling me the truth?
CISSIE 1: Yes . . .
(*A pause that brings* MADGETT *out from the sheet.*)
. . . No.
MADGETT: I feel iller still. (*He hides.*) What happened?
CISSIE 1: I drowned him in his bath.
MADGETT: God.
CISSIE 2: Come and see – it looks natural.
MADGETT: God!
CISSIE 1: You're going to help me, Madgett, now pull yourself together.
MADGETT: (*Coming out from the sheet*) I am? And what's in it for me?
CISSIE 1: (*Putting her hand on his plump belly*) Madgett, you're a coroner . . .
MADGETT: For God's sake, stop reminding me . . . but that's nice (*Referring to* CISSIE 1*'s attentions*). Try a bit lower.
CISSIE 2: Shall I leave now? While you two come to some sort of agreement?
CISSIE 1: Don't be stupid.
(SMUT *enters with a bowl of chocolate pudding and a spoon.*)
SMUT: I couldn't find any lemon juice – you'll have to have warm chocolate pudding.
(MADGETT *sits up in bed and begins to eat the pudding slowly, while* SMUT *and the two* CISSIES *stand around the bed and watch.*)
CISSIE 1: Madgett, come on . . . (*Shaking him*) Madgett.
MADGETT: Cissie – I'm in no especial hurry to assist your crimes.
CISSIE 1: Madgett, there's a corpse in my house.
MADGETT: It's only your husband.
CISSIE 1: The flies are settling on him.
MADGETT: Brush them off – use a newspaper.
CISSIE 1: Madgett! – I need legal aid, not a fly swat.

Section 10: Nancy's House

44. INT. NANCY'S HOUSE – BEDROOM. DAY
NANCY stirring in bed. A noise outside the door. Light

streaming in through the window. NANCY sits up, puzzled, blinking. CISSIE COLPITTS 3 pushes open the door and stumbles among the shoes scattered on the floor. CISSIE 3 is nineteen; she has luminous white skin and bright teeth, earrings in pierced ears. She carries a steaming saucepan and a cup.

CISSIE 3: Nancy, I heard that you were ill and I've come to see you.
NANCY: Ill? . . . God, my head.
CISSIE 3: You see. Here's something for you.
(CISSIE 3 *pours the contents of the saucepan into the cup*.)
NANCY: What is it?
CISSIE 3: Warm milk with a little lemon juice. Best drunk through a straw, but I can't find one in your kitchen.
NANCY: I don't need it.
CISSIE 3: Yes, you do and you're to take the day off, Nancy.
NANCY: Stop calling me Nancy. My Christian name is Nellie . . . and who said . . .
CISSIE 3: You were seen showing off in George Street, and peeing over a drain outside the library . . .
NANCY: God – I what?
CISSIE 3: . . . and Mrs Cunningham said you wouldn't have known a cow from a laundry van. The bed is damp, Nancy. What have you been doing?
(NANCY *bursts into tears*.)
NANCY: My God, my God.
CISSIE 3: Blasphemy always sounds real coming from a Sunday school teacher, Nancy. So you be careful.
NANCY: I remember Jake bought me a drink . . . for my birthday.
CISSIE 3: He buys everyone a drink . . . though he's just bought and drunk his last – a tubful of soapy water. He's dead . . . and you were the last to see him . . . Where are your shoes, Nancy?
NANCY: Dead? Under the bed . . . no, not those . . . in the cupboard . . . God, I don't know.

Holding her head, NANCY kneels in bed, sipping the cup contents. She discovers red paint on the back of her leg at the back of the knee, is puzzled and says nothing. CISSIE 3 goes through the clothes scattered on the bed.

CISSIE 3: You didn't leave them anywhere, did you?
NANCY: God, my shoes.
CISSIE 3: God is no cobbler. I like your knickers, Nancy.

Where did you get them?
NANCY: My name's Nellie and leave my knickers alone. (*She looks at them and bursts into tears.*) They're not mine.
CISSIE 3: Then whose are they? Do you swap underwear as easily as you swap names? (*Deliberately encouraging* NANCY's *confusion*) Nancy, what have you been doing?

Section 11: *Madgett's Car*

45. INT./EXT. MADGETT'S CAR/COUNTRY LANES. DAY

The camera at the back looking at the backs of four heads as the car travels through country lanes in the sunshine of a midsummer morning. The two CISSIE COLPITTS are seated in the back seat, MADGETT is driving and SMUT is in the front passenger seat. They are not driving very fast at all.

CISSIE 2: Why don't we go a little faster, Madgett?
SMUT: (*Calling out*) Pigeon!
MADGETT: This car doesn't like to go fast – and neither do I.
CISSIE 2: Twenty-eight miles an hour isn't remotely fast [NUMBER 28].
SMUT: (*Calling out*) Crow!
MADGETT: Surgeons travel very fast – would you like to travel with a surgeon? Doctors travel moderately fast, then vets, then coroners . . .
SMUT: (*Calling out*) Jay!
MADGETT: Did you know that there are more car accidents involving surgeons than involving coroners?
SMUT: (*Calling out*) Rabbit!
MADGETT: There are twenty-nine [NUMBER 29] surgeons to every coroner. It's about the right number . . .
(*The car passes a 30-mph road sign* (NUMBER 30).)
. . . to keep a coroner steadily employed travelling from the scene of one crashed surgeon to another . . .
SMUT: Stop!
MADGETT: Why?

46. EXT. COUNTRY LANES. DAY

During the previous scene there are five travelling shots of crushed corpses on the road as the car passes over them: a crushed pigeon, a crushed crow, a crushed jay, a crushed rabbit. Each corpse is more messy and bloody than the last. The

rabbit corpse lies in the crosspath of a scattering of paper streamers from a paperchase. The streamers issue out from a gate on one side of the road and cross the road to a track on the other side of the road. Some of the streamers have become bloodied in the guts of the corpse.
An ambiguous and very bloody animal corpse on the road. This time the camera stays with the corpse as the car swerves a little and screeches to a halt. There is a silence as the flies, disturbed by the passing car, resettle on the corpse. The car has stopped close to an isolated concrete water tower – a modern structure – gaunt and ugly, whose shadow darkens a patch of the road.

47. INT./EXT. CAR/WATER TOWER 1. DAY
Back in the car.
    MADGETT: What was it?
    SMUT: An interesting corpse.
    CISSIE 2: Oh no.
    MADGETT: Did you see what it was?
    SMUT: Unrecognizable.

48. INT./EXT. MADGETT'S CAR/WATER TOWER 1. DAY.
Seen from the outside of the car, MADGETT and SMUT get out. SMUT carries with him a small hand shovel, a can of yellow paint, a paint brush, a Polaroid camera, a notebook and a pencil on a string. MADGETT carries a map.
They walk back along the road. There is gentle birdsong and a slight breeze in the roadside cow parsley.
Inside the car, looking at the two women who are themselves looking out of the back window. The women turn to face the front. Between them through the back window can be seen the man and boy looking at the corpse on the road.
    CISSIE 2: You'd think he'd grow tired of it.
    (*She puts on red lipstick – blood red.*)
    CISSIE 1: It's just an abiding fascination . . . for a coroner.

49. EXT. CORPSE ON ROAD. DAY
The squashed ambiguous animal corpse. It has a numbered tag attached to an unidentified part of its body (NUMBER 31).
The Great Death Game
    SMUT: (*Voice over*) A great many things are dying very violently all the time. The best days for violent deaths are

Tuesdays. They are the yellow-paint days. Saturdays are second best – or worst. Saturdays are red-paint days. The Great Death Game is therefore a contest between red-paint days and yellow-paint days. So far yellow-paint days are winning by thirty-one corpses to twenty-nine. Whatever the colour, a violent death is always celebrated by a firework.

50. EXT. ROAD BY WATER TOWER 1. DAY
SMUT takes his hand shovel and lays the corpse reverently in the verge. SMUT paints a yellow circle where the corpse was, puts down an arrow and stencils a figure. MADGETT produces a map and marks it with the same figure (NUMBER 32).
SMUT takes one of CISSIE's fireworks from his pocket, props it up and lights it near the site of the corpse. MADGETT and SMUT stand back and watch it zoom up. Rooks clatter, jays scream, blackbirds scold. They walk silently back to the car. The following conversation is heard distantly but distinctly.

CISSIE 2: What was all that about?
MADGETT: We were all just celebrating an unidentifiable corpse . . . there are a lot about.
CISSIE 2: (*Mock solemnity*) Really.
CISSIE 1: Well, Madgett dear, the next one's not so unidentifiable. Got your yellow paint ready, Smut dear?
CISSIE 2: Mother!

The car drives off down the leafy sunlit lane. The yellow circle of paint shining in the foreground's dappled sunlight.

Section 12: The House of Cissie Colpitts 1

51. INT./EXT. THE HOUSE OF CISSIE COLPITTS 1 – KITCHEN/GARDEN. DAY
The two tubs of water dominate the kitchen, which is still strewn with objects just as Cissie left it. MADGETT is kneeling on the floor and examining the dead body of JAKE in the water tub. The kitchen is flooded with warm sunlight. The three CISSIEs stand together waiting for MADGETT's verdict. CISSIE 2 has her arm around her mother's shoulder. CISSIE 3 is holding CISSIE 2's arm and is resting her chin on CISSIE 1's other shoulder. They stand very still in the sunlight. MADGETT straightens and stands up, backlit water droplets fall from MADGETT's fingers. The water drops quietly splash into

the water in the tub.

MADGETT: He's dead.

CISSIE 2: God! Well done, Madgett!

CISSIE 1: And what did he die of?

MADGETT: Well . . . (*There is a pause*) . . . he drowned.

CISSIE 2: (*Mock surprise*) Did he?

MADGETT: (*Seriously*) Of course.

CISSIE 1: Why did he die?

MADGETT: (*Sniffing*) There is a strong smell of alcohol.

CISSIE 2: (*With* CISSIE 3 *giggling beside her*) So there is.

CISSIE 1: (*Frowning her disapproval at the two other* CISSIES, *and determined to keep the proceedings serious*) He drowned in his bath due to excessive drinking? (*She is trying to put words into* MADGETT's *mouth.*)

MADGETT: Unlikely. Even in the most disadvantageous circumstances. . . (*He now looks wryly at* CISSIE 1) . . . human beings have an almost involuntary desire to stay alive.

CISSIE 1: What's the answer then?

CISSIE 3: What's that?

(*There is a noise of hammering outside the window. They all turn to look.* SMUT's *arm and hand complete with a mallet is rising and falling outside the window.*)

MADGETT: (*Calmly*) Oh – it's Smut marking the spot. What's the reward?

CISSIE 1: Reward?

MADGETT: What do I get for writing out a death certificate that says 'death caused by drowning after heart attack brought on by excessive drinking'?

CISSIE 1: (*Mockingly*) Madgett – I'm appalled!

MADGETT: (*Totally unemotionally*) I see.

CISSIE 1: (*A little uncertainly*) What do you want, Madgett?

MADGETT: Well, Cissie, (*With a wry smile*) I'd have thought you would have guessed?

CISSIE 1: (*Knowing full well, but forcing him to say it*) No, you tell me!

CISSIE 2: Is this the moment when we leave the room?

MADGETT: (*Without looking at them*) Yes. The second tub needs emptying.

(*Struggling with the weight and quietly smiling at one another,* CISSIE 2 *and* CISSIE 3 *lift the second tub out of the kitchen into the garden.*)

CISSIE 1: Well?

MADGETT: Well. A little bodily comfort would be good for a start.
CISSIE 1: Madgett, I am sixty-three.
MADGETT: So?
CISSIE 1: Well – aren't I too old for you?
MADGETT: Were you too old for him?
(*The conversation takes place over the dead body of* JAKE *in the tub. They both look down at him. The sun is on his face.*)
(*With some tenderness*) Cissie – you've not been unaware of how I've felt about you.
CISSIE 1: (*Stalling but unafraid*) It's a bit soon, isn't it?
MADGETT: I could wait a little while . . .
CISSIE 1: I think you'd have to – to stop tongues wagging.
MADGETT: . . . but not too long.
CISSIE 1: (*Smiling*) This is blackmail.
MADGETT: (*Smiling back*) Yes.

52. EXT. THE HOUSE OF CISSIE COLPITTS 1 – SIDE. DAY
Round the side of the house, CISSIE 2 and CISSIE 3 empty the tub of water over the garden. The water splashes out in the sunlight. To one side SMUT is carefully spray-painting with yellow paint and a stencil the number 33 (NUMBER 33) on the stake he has hammered into the ground. The two women creep up on SMUT and, grabbing him by the armpits, hoist him into the air and kiss him on both cheeks.
CISSIE 2: Smut! Which are you first – a ghoul or a mathematician?
SMUT: Neither – I'm just a clerk.
CISSIE 3: (*Laughing*) How modest!

Section 13: The House of Cissie Colpitts 1

53. EXT. THE HOUSE OF CISSIE COLPITTS 1 – FIELD. DAY
On the field outside CISSIE 1's house – CISSIE 1, CISSIE 2, CISSIE 3, SMUT, MADGETT, HARDY and CISSIE 3's boyfriend, BELLAMY, play one of MADGETT's games. A wide shot establishes the seven players in a circle in the foreground with CISSIE 1's house in the background. The early morning has turned into a beautiful day with bright sunlight. The field is full of buttercups.
The game is a form of Handicap Catch. The players throw an

object around in a circle. If a player drops it, the next time he
or she must catch it with one hand, then on one knee, then on
two knees, then in his or her lap . . . if this fails the player is
out. Madgett's game starts by throwing a red skittle, which is
joined by two more red skittles and then a black one. The out
or 'dead' players lie on a sheet on the ground in the centre of
the circle.

BELLAMY, aged about twenty-three, is resentfully a participant
and HARDY, CISSIE 2's husband, is reluctant. They are poor
players.

As before, SMUT, in voice over, reads out the rules of the game.
His description is careful, thorough and methodical.

Deadman's Catch

   SMUT: (*Voice over*) If a player in the game of Deadman's
   Catch drops a skittle, he is obliged to suffer a succession of
   handicaps. First to catch using one hand, then to catch
   kneeling on one knee, then on two knees, then with one eye
   closed. If a player finally drops a catch with both eyes closed,
   then he is out and must take his place in the winding-sheet.

It is not absolutely essential to comprehend the details of the
game – they are largely self-evident anyway – the important
thing to stress is SMUT's obsessive concern for game-playing,
and to glimpse some metaphorical significance regarding the
position and future of the various characters.

   HARDY: Madgett, what sort of game is this?
   MADGETT: One to be played with skill.
   BELLAMY: Some skill – it's a kid's game. (*He drops a skittle.*)
   Damn – that was a lousy throw, Smut.
   CISSIE 3: Stop complaining and use one hand.

Behind them, two UNDERTAKERS struggle out of the back door
of CISSIE 1's house with a heavy bath of water. They pour it on
the flowers beside the back door and go back inside. The
players do not turn around, being intent on the game.

   HARDY: Madgett, this is no time to play games, what will
   everybody think?
   CISSIE 2: Let them think what they like.
   HARDY: You can see Cissie's upset.
   CISSIE 3: Then it's best to keep her mind occupied . . . down
   on one knee, Bellamy.
   BELLAMY: These are my best trousers – I came to pay my
   respects.
   CISSIE 3: (*Laughing*) So you can pay your respects kneeling.

Further over on the field, SID THE DIGGER – previously seen when the two CISSIES were wheeling NANCY's body – unobtrusively approaches, stays his distance and sits in the grass and buttercups, and, taking out an oily rag, begins to polish his shiny spade. SMUT every now and then gives him a glance. The women play strongly, the men with difficulty. HARDY drops twice and goes down on one knee.

HARDY: I can't spend all my time playing games, Cissie.

CISSIE 1: What's your time worth, Hardy? I was married to Jake for thirty-four years [NUMBER 34]. Surely you can spare him a few minutes.

SMUT: Is he going to be buried or cremated, Cissie?

CISSIE 1: Cremated.

SMUT: And where are you going to scatter his ashes?

CISSIE 1: Oh – don't worry – I'll find a suitable place for those.

HARDY: Cissie – you're hard-hearted.

(*He drops a catch.*)

CISSIE 2: And you're a lousy catch. No eyes and no hands! (*Behind them, the* UNDERTAKERS *struggle out with* JAKE's *coffin.* HARDY *fails to catch a black skittle in his lap and he's out.*)

SMUT: Into the winding sheet, Hardy. You're dead.

BELLAMY: God – you're a little ghoul, Smut. Who's your father? Blast it!

(BELLAMY *drops a catch. As* HARDY *lies down in the white sheet, so the* UNDERTAKERS *carrying the coffin have a struggle getting the coffin through the garden gate.*)

CISSIE 1: No hands, Bellamy.

BELLAMY: All right, all right. (*He drops the black skittle.*) You did that on purpose, Smut.

CISSIE 2: Into the sheet, Bellamy – it's only a game.

HARDY: The way Madgett plays it, you'd think it meant something.

MADGETT: Well, of course it does.

CISSIE 2: It means you're a lousy catch.

MADGETT drops a catch and BELLAMY goes to lie in the sheet as the UNDERTAKERS struggle to get JAKE's coffin into the back of the hearse. HARDY and BELLAMY lie stretched out in the sun on the white sheet (like figures in Brueghel's *Harvest* or *Cockaigne*). Their presence in the sheet, of course, is significant for the future. The three CISSIES play on strongly, like three Graces or

Furies against the sky. The two UNDERTAKERS and a police coroner stare at the game-players.
>CISSIE 3: (*Eyeing* CISSIE 1) So Madgett, what is your verdict?
>MADGETT: (*Dropping a catch and preparing to catch with one hand*) Accidental death, of course.
>CISSIE 2: Are you normally left-handed?
>MADGETT: (*Looking at* CISSIE 1) Only when I write out death certificates.

In the background, the watchers climb into their vehicles and the vehicles leave. The players play in silence, SMUT and MADGETT rapidly lose their catches. SMUT is out first, soon to be followed by MADGETT. They both lie in the sheet. The women play on strongly. With two skittles – one red and one black. In the background SID THE DIGGER comes through the garden gate, leans on it, polishing his spade. SMUT is taking Polaroid photos from his position in the sheet.

Section 14: The Skipping Girl's House

54. EXT. SKIPPING GIRL'S HOUSE. DAY
Hot afternoon. SMUT sits with the SKIPPING GIRL on her step. They are surrounded by books. She sits on her chair, he sits on the step. He has spread out the Polaroid photos of the Handicap Catch on the door carpet. The GIRL is a little more elaborately dressed than the last time we saw her.
>SMUT: I've found you three more stars . . . Cygni Beta, Castor Minor and Groombridge 35 [NUMBER 35] . . . there in the North (SMUT *stands and points*) between the Twins and Ursa Minor . . . over by Cissie's house . . .
>(*A* MIDDLE-AGED MAN *comes to the door, smiles and, stepping over the children, enters. The* SKIPPING GIRL *looks at him, appraises him.*)
>. . . why don't you skip on the pavement – there's more room?
>(*She shakes her head.*)
>GIRL: (*With complete innocence*) Are you circumcised?
>(*A* SECOND MAN *comes down the corridor behind the children and walks down the street.*)
>SMUT: What's that?
>GIRL: A piece of your willie is cut off. It's in the Bible. (*She taps a thick Bible beside her chair.*) My mother . . . (*Indicating*

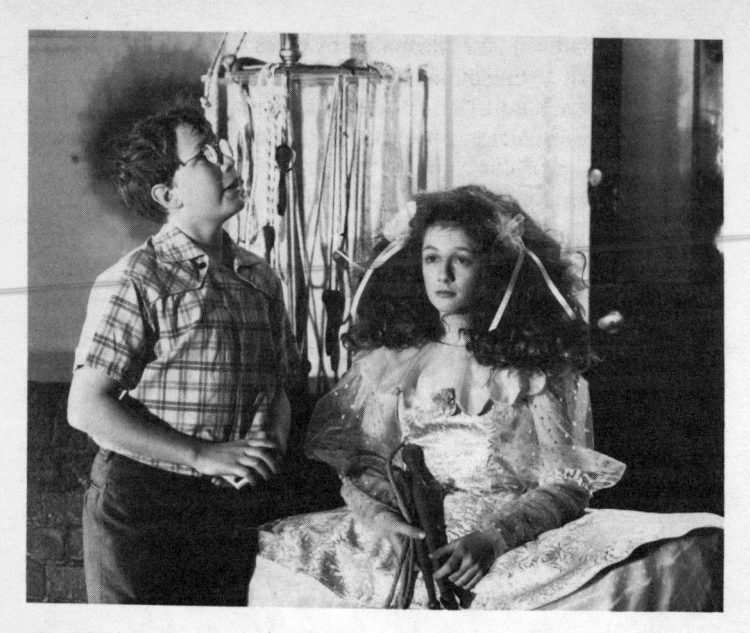

with her head the room above) . . . *says it's better that way.*
SMUT: Oh.
(*There's a pause.*)
These are the photos of Madgett's game for taking Jake to the funeral parlour.
(*He spreads them out . . . there are numerous photos of the three* CISSIES *playing the game against the sky.*)
GIRL: Who's that?
(*She points to a photo of* BELLAMY *lying on the sheet looking dead.*)
SMUT: It's Cissie's boyfriend – his name is Bellamy.
GIRL: Bellamy?
SMUT: Yes.
GIRL: On his deathbed, Prime Minister Pitt said, 'I think I could eat one of Bellamy's pork pies.'

Section 15: Picnic – Cissie 3 and Bellamy

55. EXT. LAKE. DAY
Pork pies, beer cans, crisps and apples – a modest picnic is laid out on the grass.

A country pond – a lake. Secluded by trees and screened by bushes. CISSIE 3, finishing a swim, is coming out of the water. Turning her back on BELLAMY who is sitting in the long grass watching her, she strips out of her wet costume. Her costume is numbered 36 in bright colours (NUMBER 36).
BELLAMY is eating a pork pie. Cissie dries herself in a large towel. BELLAMY makes his sexual approaches.

CISSIE 3: No . . . not that way.
(*She turns her back on him.*)
BELLAMY: (*Hesitant*) What's that fat Maggot all about?
CISSIE 3: His name is Madgett. Don't you like him?
BELLAMY: Why does everyone have to play his games?
CISSIE 3: They don't have to – but they like to. He's amusing.
BELLAMY: God, he's boring . . . like all your other friends. Like your aunt . . . and I can't believe that Jake drowned in a bath tub. When are you going to break away from that lot and come and live with me?
CISSIE 3: (*Laughing at his petulance*) I'll marry you on two conditions.
BELLAMY: What are they?
CISSIE 3: That you learn to swim . . . and (*Seriously*) never, never take me from the front. I've told you before.
BELLAMY: Why the hell not?
CISSIE 3: Because . . . I can't stand being lain on. It's too conventional and it gives me claustrophobia . . . and you won't hurt the baby.
BELLAMY: What baby?
CISSIE 3: That scared you, didn't it?
BELLAMY: What baby?
CISSIE 3: There's no baby, you dope – though the way you go about it – I'm constantly surprised.
BELLAMY: Very well – I'll agree on two conditions . . . that you stop wearing swimsuits – and you stop seeing those women.
CISSIE 3: What difference does it make to you what I wear and who I see? . . . Fancy a plumber not being able to swim. What's water for?
BELLAMY: Drinking perhaps?
CISSIE 3: I'll swap you one of the conditions – I'll stop wearing swimsuits, if you start wearing them.

Section 16: The House of Cissie Colpitts 1

56. INT. THE HOUSE OF CISSIE COLPITTS 1 – BEDROOM. DAY
Between sunset and dusk.
CISSIE 1 is combing her long hair in her bedroom at night. The mirrors are set so that she can see her front and back. A light on the table in front of her is the sole illumination. Slowly she takes her nightdress off and sits looking at herself with some curiosity. The image takes much from Rembrandt's portraits of his second wife; warm browns, bright illuminated whites and deep blacks. A clatter of small stones hits a window pane. CISSIE 1 looks sideways. She holds her nightdress to herself, gets up, smiles and looks out.

CISSIE 2: (*Heard from the garden*) Mother . . . are you all right?
CISSIE 1: (*Opening the window, holding the nightdress to her chest*) Yes, of course I'm all right.
CISSIE 2: I couldn't get in – that's the first time I ever remember you locking the front door.
CISSIE 1: Well, I'm on my own tonight. Here's the key.
(*She throws the key out into the darkness, it rings on the paved path.*)
CISSIE 2: God, Mother, you're a lousy shot.
(*Laughter.* CISSIE 1 *moves away from the window and, taking a last look at her naked self in the mirror, puts her nightdress back on.* CISSIE 2 *comes into the room.*)
It's early yet, what are you doing?
CISSIE 1: I've never been to bed before midnight for eighteen years so I thought I'd see what it was like. I was just looking at myself to see what I was worth.
CISSIE 2: Mother!
CISSIE 1: Well, since your father died, I've never – surprising as it might be to you – I've never had a good look. Jake was intimidating. The last time I had a good look was when your father was alive thirty-seven years ago [NUMBER 37].
(CISSIE 2 *laughs loudly.*)
I've moved into the single bed already . . . please remember that single beds are only meant for one . . .
(*She half sings the nursery song that* NANCY *sang at the start of the film.*)

CISSIE 2: Well – put your clothes back on again, your long-standing admirer Madgett is taking us for a drive.

Section 17: Madgett's Trysting Field

57. INT./EXT. CAR/MADGETT'S FIELD. NIGHT
A moonlit night. The Madgett car is parked in a field. All four doors of the car are open – it's a very warm night and an orange reading light illuminates the interior. CISSIE 1 sits in the driving seat. CISSIE 2 sits in the front passenger seat with her legs dangling out of the car on to the grass. CISSIE 3 is identically placed in the back-seat. Madgett and Smut are out with a torch, catching moths. We occasionally see them crouched in the grass with the flashlight and an entomological textbook. The coloured drawings of insects in the textbook are marked with Fig. 38 and Fig. 39 (NUMBERS 38 and 39).
The car looks like a beetle with its wing-cases open for flight.
   CISSIE 3: All right, Cissie, why did you do it?
   CISSIE 1: (*Dismissively, as though the point is unimportant*) He was unfaithful.
   CISSIE 3: (*Gently*) Cissie . . . He's been unfaithful before . . . why did you wait until now?

CISSIE 1: Because . . . because he'd stopped washing his feet . . . because he wouldn't cut his beard . . . because he had a hairy backside, because . . . I didn't kill him, he drowned . . . (*Long pause*) . . . I drowned him.

MADGETT and SMUT are crouched in the torch light, looking at a beetle – a stag beetle with its wing-cases open for flight. Close-up of beetle in the collecting sheet. Wide shot of car with the women standing in the field. The women's voices heard distantly, but distinctly.

CISSIE 3: Was it easy?
CISSIE 1: Yes.
CISSIE 3: He wasn't bad-looking, was he?
CISSIE 1: No – he got better as he got older.
CISSIE 2: And his conquests got younger.

MADGETT and SMUT are pulling at some unseen object in the hedge – MADGETT is holding his nose and grimacing – the inference is that they have found a corpse – some sort of animal.

CISSIE 1: How old is Nancy?
CISSIE 2: Twenty-three.
CISSIE 3: Older than me . . . and bigger tits.
CISSIE 1: What does that mean?

CISSIE 3: It means that Jake made a play for me once.
CISSIE 1: He what?
CISSIE 2: And me.
CISSIE 1: (*After a long pause*) The dirty old man . . . why have you told me now?
CISSIE 2: It might help.
CISSIE 1: (*Her final statement on the subject*) I didn't like him.
CISSIE 3: But is that sufficient reason to drown him?
CISSIE 1: Madgett says it is.
CISSIE 2: That is pretty irresponsible for a coroner.
CISSIE 1: Isn't it? If you ask him nicely, he might be irresponsible enough to help you.
CISSIE 2: What does that mean, Mother?

Startling them, a brilliant white, blue and green rocket sweeps into the sky from the position where MADGETT and SMUT were last seen. The women curse and laugh. The firework stars die away.

CISSIE 3: Lose one, win one.
CISSIE 2: What?
CISSIE 3: (*Shrugging her shoulders*) A husband. I've got some news for you. Bellamy and me – or is it I? – have decided on the thirty-first of this month – it's a Saturday.
CISSIE 2: You don't look too excited by it.
CISSIE 3: (*Impishly*) Madgett will be pleased for me.
CISSIE 1: He least of all.
CISSIE 3: I want a baby.
CISSIE 2: At nineteen? Cissie, you're mad. I thought you wanted to spend your life swimming, not bearing children.

CISSIE 1: Bellamy can't even swim – I don't think he can change a light bulb – can he?
CISSIE 3: I know . . . I know. Championship women swimmers always have their sons early.
CISSIE 2: (*Laughing and putting her hand around* CISSIE 3's *shoulder*) They do? And how sure are you that it'll be a boy?
CISSIE 1: Capable women normally have girls.
(*They all laugh.*)

Section 18: Madgett's House

58. INT. MADGETT'S HOUSE – MADGETT'S BEDROOM. NIGHT

Dark browns and warm blacks save for the area of the bed, which is just white sheets illuminated by a bedside lamp. MADGETT is sitting on the bed, propped up on white pillows. He is naked save for a brightly coloured striped woollen tie around his neck, loosely knotted. He holds a large volume – it's heavy, with marbled covers. He's resting a sheet of writing paper on it, where the first hand-written words are 'Dear Cissie . . .' It's a warm night – MADGETT looks like an overwarm Silenus. On the wall behind his head is a reproduction of Brueghel's *Children's Games*.

A diminutive ghost enters from the left-hand side, a small agile figure under a crisp sheet that trails the floor. It is SMUT. Momentarily, MADGETT is beside himself with fright. Then, resignedly and completely without anger, he realizes it is SMUT. SMUT is carrying a large art book under the sheet.

MADGETT: Smut, what do you want?
SMUT: (*Taking off the sheet*) I'm hot and is it true that it's desirable to be circumcised in a hot climate?
MADGETT: So they say.
SMUT: (*Placing the book open at a* Samson and Delilah *reproduction on the bed*) Was Samson circumcised?
(*The book is open at page 40* (NUMBER 40).)
MADGETT: Yes, so were Christ, Marx, Freud and Einstein.
SMUT: Does it hurt?
MADGETT: I don't remember.
SMUT: What does it look like?
MADGETT: It's nothing special. Look. (*He shows him.*) Now go to bed.
SMUT: Was Delilah circumcised? Do they circumcise women?
MADGETT: Sort of . . . in hot countries.
SMUT: It's hot here.
MADGETT: So it is.
SMUT: Did they do it to Cissie?
MADGETT: I doubt it very much.
SMUT: Was Jake circumcised?
MADGETT: You'd better ask Cissie.
SMUT: Is circumcision barbaric?
MADGETT: Some say so. Now get back to bed, and anything unanswered about the barbarity of men to women you can ask Cissie in the morning – she's an authority. Now let me write.

SMUT pulls the sheet back over his head and, walking like a ghost, sleepwalks out of the bedroom. At the same moment a gust of wind sweeps in from the open windows on the right of frame. It blows the long white curtains into the air and ruffles the thin pages of MADGETT's book.

MADGETT gets out of bed to close the window. He carries the letter he was writing. Plump, naked and vulnerable, he stands there a moment, staring out into the night. There is a faint bellowing – an ambiguous noise – perhaps a field away – a wounded noise, accompanied by more familiar noises of distant curlews. He slowly rips the letter up in small pieces and throws them out of the window.

59. EXT. MADGETT'S HOUSE. NIGHT

Cut to an outside view of the Madgett house. MADGETT seen at the lit window in the moonless night, the white pieces of paper flickering down, caught by the beam of window light. As MADGETT turns away from his window so SMUT comes to his and opens it. There is a whispered conversation.

    SMUT: Number forty-one [NUMBER 41] is by the bridge in Cattermole Road.

A polished spade flashes in the light, identifying the person in the garden as SID THE DIGGER. SMUT throws him down a map and a notebook. SID picks them up, touches his hat and disappears in the dark. SMUT closes his window and draws the curtain.

Section 19: Madgett's House

60. EXT. MADGETT'S HOUSE. EARLY MORNING

The Beginnings of the Pursuit. It's early morning outside Madgett's house. MADGETT is wearing a dressing-gown. With bare feet and tousled hair he is standing on the front strip of grass. He is batting a tennis ball around on a post – a conventional game of Swing Ball. There is evidence that the paperchase has travelled across a corner of the lawn. In the background of the garden, TEIGAN is carrying and arranging chairs on the lawn under the apple trees. SMUT, fully dressed and wearing a bee-keeper's hat, comes out of the house, eating a piece of honey-spread toast. He takes a newspaper out of a red drainage pipe wedged in the hedge and begins to open it up.

    SMUT: Here it is. 'Jake Grenideer died of a heart attack in his bath. He was sixty-five. Said the coroner, "It was a very comfortable place to die." ' Did you say that, Madgett? 'His widow, Mrs Cissie Grenideer, née Colpitts, said, "He didn't bath very often." ' Did Cissie really say that?

While SMUT has been reading, NANCY and her brother GREGORY have come quietly up the beach road and are standing at a hesitant distance waiting for a chance to be noticed. NANCY hangs back.

    GREGORY: Madgett . . . we've a bone to pick with you.
    MADGETT: Come and pick it, Gregory. Smut, make some tea. Bring it out the front. Nancy, sit here.

    (*He sweeps various yellow-painted stencils off the table – some*

are still sticky and the paint comes off on his fingers – one of the stencils bears the number 42 (NUMBER 42).)
GREGORY: We're not stopping, Madgett – you'll get us playing some game we can't afford. It's about Jake.
MADGETT: (*Surreptitiously trying to wipe the yellow paint off his fingers into the newspaper left on the table by* SMUT) What about him?
GREGORY: Nancy thinks . . . has dreamt . . . is worried . . . that he might not have died through natural causes.
MADGETT: Good lord. What makes you think that, Nancy?
GREGORY: She had red paint on her leg.
(SMUT *brings out the tea on a tray, puts it on the table and goes off down the garden to the hives which can be seen from the front of the house.*)
MADGETT: Pardon?
NANCY: I had red paint on my leg when I got up yesterday.
MADGETT: Perhaps it was blood – have you been bleeding lately, Nancy?
GREGORY: And she can't find her shoes.
MADGETT: Does this add up to an unnatural death in a bath tub?
GREGORY: It might.
MADGETT: How might it? I can't see it.
GREGORY: Nor can I, Madgett – but Nancy says she can.
(*Down the garden,* SMUT *is jumping about.*)
What's he doing?
MADGETT: He's counting the bees.
GREGORY: (NANCY's *problems forgotten*) Why's he doing that?
MADGETT: Oh – he's always counting something.
GREGORY: (*Pouring himself a cup of tea and nodding at the bees*) Has the hive been told? Bees should be told about a death.
MADGETT: It only applies to blood relatives, doesn't it?
GREGORY: (*Mischievously*) Isn't she going to be a blood relative?
MADGETT: Isn't who?
GREGORY: Cissie, Jake's widow.
MADGETT: Gregory, what makes you think that?
GREGORY: (*Grinning*) Isn't that why you signed the death certificate 'heart attack'?
MADGETT: Good Lord, Gregory. What an imagination.
GREGORY: (*Seriously said*) I know. I got it from my mother.

MADGETT: (*As seriously*) Mothers have a lot to answer for.
(GREGORY *manages to get yellow paint on the back of his hand.*)
I'm sorry – it's Smut. Have a newspaper.
(GREGORY *attempts to wipe his hands on the newspaper.*
MADGETT *looks at his watch and shouts down the garden.*)
Smut, you're late, you're supposed to be swimming. (*He takes* GREGORY *by the shoulder.*) Gregory, come and try this game out with me – you too, Nancy.
NANCY: I've got to go. (*She grabs* GREGORY *by the sleeve.*) You've forgot to tell Madgett about my . . .
(*She hesitates and then whispers the final word in* GREGORY's *ear.*)
GREGORY: He doesn't want to know about them. Silly girl . . .
MADGETT: (*To an angry, embarrassed and crestfallen* NANCY) All right, Nancy, see you later then. Mind the sheep.

61. EXT. MADGETT'S HOUSE – SIDE. EARLY MORNING
MADGETT steers GREGORY around the side of the house. They both step carefully over the trail of papers from the paperchase. Ten dining chairs are laid out in a pattern on the grass. The chairs, under the trees, throw sharp shadows on the white wall of the house. On a stool set aside from the chairs is a wind-up gramophone. As NANCY steers her way gingerly through the sheep to the front gate and SMUT leaves the hives, TEIGAN winds up the gramophone. The music plays – a German funeral march – NANCY slams the gate, SMUT throws his bee-gloves down on to a chair and walks into the house. He is talking to himself under his bee-hat.
Bees in the Trees
SMUT: The game of Bees in the Trees is a variant of musical chairs and is best played with funeral music and in the open air. The object of the game is to sit down on a vacant chair when the music stops. If the chair sat on is occupied by bees, it is permissible to arrange a professional foul . . .
SMUT's commentary is wry. It trails off deliberately and there is no way of knowing exactly what the game is about.
MADGETT and GREGORY waltz around the chairs, the music stops and MADGETT pushes GREGORY into a chair and then knocks the chair and GREGORY to the ground. GREGORY, surprised, sprawls on the grass. MADGETT and TEIGAN laugh and, taking his cue from MADGETT but not fully realizing why,

GREGORY laughs too. Their laughter is cut short when they start to flap and dodge a crowd of buzzing bees. The whole of the incident is seen in long-shot on a beautiful warm summer morning.

Section 20: Swimming Baths

62. INT. SWIMMING BATHS. DAY
CISSIE 3, with the number 43 (NUMBER 43) on her swimming cap, swims luxuriously, sensuously and very skilfully in the blue-tinged water of a municipal swimming pool. She knows she is good, delights in it, even triumphs in it. Every now and then, she passes SMUT who swims with a snorkel. Reaching the shallow end on a swimming length, CISSIE 3 momentarily pauses for breath and is confronted by two quite hefty middle-aged men with ginger hair.
    JONAH: Are you Cissie Colpitts?
    CISSIE 3: (*A little surprised*) Yes I am – though there are others.
    JONAH: Our name is Bognor – B O G N O R. I'm Jonah and this is Moses.
    MOSES: We are cousins of the dead man.
    CISSIE 3: (*Genuinely forgotten*) What dead man?
    MOSES: Come on – don't be stupid. Jake, of course.
Their manner is aggressive. All three are submerged up to their necks in water that is constantly being rocked and splashed by passing swimmers. Most lively among the swimmers is SMUT who wears a snorkel.
    CISSIE 3: (*Thinking fast*) Pleased to meet you. Are you in training too?
    JONAH: Training?
    CISSIE 3: (*Disingenuously*) For the Olympics.
    JONAH: No . . . are you?
    CISSIE 3: (*Brightly*) Oh yes. There are my coaches. Over there.
CISSIE 3 indicates two women sitting on the pool edge, deep in conversation. They are both wearing swimming costumes and sit surrounded by towels and clothes. One wears a red beret. The two women are CISSIE 1 and CISSIE 2.
    CISSIE 3: The woman in the red beret trained Dawn Fraser. The other one swam with Esther Williams in Stockholm.

MOSES: I thought Esther Williams was a singer.
Taking advantage of their momentary confusion, CISSIE 3 edges and then swims away from the two men whose manner was threatening. They look at one another. CISSIE 3 swims towards the other two CISSIES. The men move to the opposite side and ease themselves up on to the pool edge.
CISSIE 3 eases herself out of the water at the feet of CISSIES 1 and 2. CISSIE 2 hands CISSIE 3 a towel.

CISSIE 3: Cissie, do you know those two men?
CISSIE 1: (*Looking*) No . . . wait a minute . . . they look vaguely familiar . . . perhaps it's the beards.
CISSIE 3: They know you.
CISSIE 1: They do?
CISSIE 3: They're Jake's cousins. They're called Moses and Jonah.
CISSIE 1: Good watery connections.
(*The two bearded swimmers pass close to the three seated Colpitts women – they stare hard at them.* CISSIE 3 *makes play with some 'coach' talk.*)
CISSIE 3: How much do you think body hair is appreciably responsible for extra drag, Miss Freilichberg?
CISSIE 1: Pardon?
CISSIE 3: Do you think I ought to shave, and not just my legs? What would I look like bald, do you think?
CISSIE 1: What?
CISSIE 2: What do Bellamy and you get up to?
CISSIE 3: You two make a pair of lousy swimming coaches. (*Doing a heavy nudge in the direction of* JAKE'S *cousins*) When I need to impress, I expect support.
CISSIE 2: Sorry – at the turn, it's essential that the muscles of the pelvis move forty-five degrees at an angle to the trunk – Johnny Weissmuller said that . . .
CISSIE 3: All right, all right, too late . . .
(SMUT *walks around the bath.*)
CISSIE 1: Smut, is this your towel?
(*She shakes the towel and bees fall out.*)
CISSIES 1 and 2: God!
(SMUT *catches the bees – some of them, as they walk stunned on the poolside tiles – and examines three of them closely.*)
SMUT: It's all right, these have been counted. This is number forty-four [NUMBER 44].

63. INT. SWIMMING BATHS. DAY
Close-up of a wet, stunned bee in SMUT's palm.

Section 21: Bellamy's Kitchen

64. INT. BELLAMY'S KITCHEN. DAY
A neon light-strip in an adjacent room flickers irregularly – though it is bright daylight outside the neon still makes a significant flicker. There is a number 45 on the dresser (NUMBER 45).
CISSIE 3 is lying face down on an apple-green PVC tablecloth on the kitchen table. Her hair is still damp and frizzed from the pool. She makes swimming actions of the crawl with her arms and legs. BELLAMY, sitting on a chair, has his head and hands under her full skirt.

CISSIE 3: . . . then you draw your arms to your sides . . . are you watching?
BELLAMY: Yes, in detail. You smell of chlorine.
CISSIE 3: (*Laughing*) Do you like it?
BELLAMY: It tastes salty.
CISSIE 3: (*Laughing and squirming*) That's not the chlorine you dope, that's me. Are you coming to the funeral?
BELLAMY: Am I invited?
CISSIE 3: I'll invite you, and after, you can come swimming.
BELLAMY: I'm not fooling around in a bath full of kids and their mums on a Saturday afternoon.
CISSIE 3: You want to see Jake off, don't you?
BELLAMY: I hardly knew him. Open your legs again.
CISSIE 3: Liar. You drank with him often enough.
BELLAMY: Enough to know he was hen-pecked . . . And enough to know that he would be the last to drown, for God's sake, in eighteen inches of soapy water.
CISSIE 3: He wasn't very clean, was he? This tablecloth's sticky. As an official competitor I can get free time in the bath.
BELLAMY: Official competitor in what?
CISSIE 3: I can get a key. Olympic Trials – women's breast stroke. We can have the pool to ourselves.
BELLAMY: Olympic Trials? Pull the other one.
CISSIE 3: I thought that that was what you were doing? You push the knees out and you pull the knees in . . . in a pincer

movement (*She grips his head tightly between her knees.*) It's probably like having a baby.

Section 22: Crematorium 1

65. EXT. CREMATORIUM I. DAY
A service is being conducted in the open air. Wreaths and flowers are laid out around a group of mourners, the flowers contained in numbered plots by tasselled ropes. Plot numbers 46 and 47 are in evidence – discreetly (NUMBERS 46 and 47). The three CISSIE COLPITTS are lined up beside the coffin of JAKE. Behind them are BELLAMY, HARDY, MADGETT and SMUT. NANCY and JAKE's cousins – JONAH and MOSES – are a little further off, with a marked distance between them and the major mourners. GREGORY and TEIGAN are a little further off still. They all face front – like figures in a formal group photograph. SMUT has his Polaroid camera around his neck – he takes surreptitious photos. There are a great many cut flowers – essentially country flowers – it looks as though most of them come from CISSIE I's garden. The officiating PRIEST is off-screen.

    CISSIE 2: You know why they built the crematorium here, don't you?
    CISSIE 3: No.
    CISSIE 2: The ground is so waterlogged around here that you can't dig a grave without making a pond. Ask Sid. As it is, they hold these services at low tide, in case the water puts the fire out.
    CISSIE 3: (*Giggling and sharply nudging* CISSIE 2) Cissie!
    CISSIE 1: Here comes the bit I've never liked.
    (*The officiating* PRIEST *drones the last words of the service.*)
    CISSIE 2: Bite your lip and try counting . . . in threes.
    CISSIE 1: That's too easy.
    (*The three women start to count in threes,* 3 6 9 – 12 15 18 – 21 24 27 – 30 33 36 – 39 42 45 – *and* CISSIE 1 *ends up with* 48 (NUMBER 48). *She stops because she realizes she is being overheard. Despite efforts to the contrary,* CISSIE 1 *weeps.*)
    JONAH: What are they doing?
    NANCY: They're counting. They often do it.
    (*Hearing this comment,* CISSIE 1 *hides her face behind a large bunch of orange calceolarias.*)

JONAH: Are you the local coroner?
MADGETT: I am.
MOSES: How come a 6-foot man dies in a 4-foot bath?
MADGETT: He died of a heart attack.
JONAH: A bit inconvenient to have a heart attack in a bath, isn't it?
MADGETT: It's a bit inconvenient to have a heart attack anywhere.
MOSES: What would you say if we said we didn't agree with your verdict?
MADGETT: I would say that you'd better find me some evidence to the contrary.
JONAH: Well – how about 'Why were there two baths?' – eh, Madgett?
(*Before he can say anything else, four brightly coloured rockets zoom up from among the flowers. Everyone is startled.*)
CISSIE 1: For God's sake, Cissie, you must stop giving that boy fireworks.
CISSIE 2: Why? It's good for business.

Section 23: Madgett's Car

66. INT./EXT. MADGETT'S CAR/WATER TOWER 1
The return from the cemetery.
At mid-evening two hours from sunset. In Madgett's car, the three CISSIES sit crushed together in the back seat. SMUT sits beside MADGETT in the front. The women look enigmatic, slightly unreal and very handsome.
From a distance, glimpsed through the trees along the road, is the concrete water tower that has been glimpsed once or twice before. It grows larger as the car approaches it – a white, looming feature, incongruous and ugly. MADGETT, not travelling fast, slows down because two cars have been badly parked on the narrow lane, one on each side. Four people are standing just off the road near the base of the water tower. They are NANCY, JAKE's cousins and BELLAMY. They all watch as the Madgett car passes. The COLPITTS in the back of Madgett's car stare out of the window.
There is a graffiti slogan on the water tower concrete base that contains the number 49 (NUMBER 49).
CISSIE 2: Look who's there – Nancy . . .

CISSIE 1: . . . and those two swimmers from the bath . . .
CISSIE 3: . . . and Bellamy.
MADGETT: (*Laughing*) Perhaps there's a conspiracy.
CISSIE 1: A conspiracy?
MADGETT: How about the Water Tower Conspiracy? Set to accuse you, Cissie, of drowning.
CISSIE 1: Rubbish! You're not serious.
(*The car has passed the obstruction, but the water tower still looms significantly through the back window and in the driving mirrors.*)
MADGETT: Well . . . I had a sort of complaint yesterday from Nancy . . . she came to me to complain of red paint on her leg, lost shoes, and some other, I gather . . . embarrassing missing article.
SMUT: (*Nonchalantly*) Her knickers.
MADGETT: Really?
CISSIE 1: (*Laughing*) How do you know that?
SMUT: She paid me to go into your kitchen and look for them.
CISSIE 1: She what?
SMUT: (*Unperturbed*) Well, she used to be my Sunday School teacher.

CISSIE 2: I suppose Jake could look like a lascivious Old Testament prophet.
CISSIE 1: Sshh!
SMUT: She taught me the Ten Commandments – not to lie . . .
CISSIE 2: . . . not to commit adultery . . .
CISSIE 1: Shut up, Cissie.
SMUT: And I found them on the floor under the sink and I put them in my pocket and I told her they weren't there – which was true because they were in my pocket.
And here they are. (*With an undemonstrative flourish, he takes them out of his pocket*) And it'll cost each of you another 50p [NUMBER 50].
CISSIE 3: God, Smut, that showed great presence of mind.
CISSIE 2: (*Laughing*) And a taste for business.
(CISSIE 1 *leans over the front seat and kisses* SMUT *on the cheek.*)
CISSIE 1: Well then, that settles it, if I go down, it looks as if you'll all go down with me.

67. INT./EXT. MADGETT'S CAR/SKIPPING GIRL'S HOUSE. DAY
The car, now in a gradually increasingly built-up area, passes the row of terraced houses where the SKIPPING GIRL lives. She is sitting in her corridor doorway, asleep on a large wooden chair. A glass of milk on a plate stands before her on a stool. The skipping rope is held tightly in her hands.

Section 24: The House of Cissie 2

68. EXT. THE HOUSE OF CISSIE 2 – BEACH. DAY
The Middle Game.
There is a celebration for the marriage of CISSIE 3 and 'SPLASH' BELLAMY. On the foreshore are tables and chairs, flags and food. There are deckchairs on the veranda in front of the house, bathing costumes, towels, beach umbrellas. Round the side of the house are parked cars with white wedding ribbons.
On the beach itself, in the brilliant late-afternoon sunshine, a crowd of people, as nearly naked as decency permits, are playing a game akin to French Cricket, which has numerous

embellishments devised by MADGETT and executed by SMUT. The object of the game is to strike the batsman below the knee – everyone has either a red ribbon, or a red line painted just below the knee. The masks and hats identify the players as characters from numerous games, folklore, Punch and Judy shows, the fairground and so on – thus: the Fat Lady, the Dunce, the Emperor, the Hangman, the Ghost, the Banker, the Cripple, etc. The game is played with great enthusiasm and noise in a rush of movement in and out of the sea.

The sequence opens with a mêlée of medium close-ups and close-ups of ambiguous moves, gestures, throws, catches, running feet, suggestive areas of flesh, strange falls, snatches of aggression, sand in the mouth, pulled swimsuits, barking dogs and spurts of sand.

Hangman's Cricket

   SMUT: (*Voice over*) The object of Hangman's Cricket is for each competitor to retain his allotted nine lives by scoring runs with the Cat, or bat, defending his lower leg from being struck by the ball. There is no limit to the number of players as long as each has an identity agreed by the two referees. Each identity has its own characteristic which must be obeyed. The more important identities are the Emperor, the Widow, the Judge, the Hangman, the Ghost, the Red Queen, the Fat Lady, the Dunce, the Businessman, the Adulterer, the Harlot, the Gravedigger, the Maiden, the Twins, the Chinaman, the Savage, the Cook, the General, the Prisoner, the Beggarman, the Thief and the Priest.

SMUT continues to explain the rules over the following scenes – his careful voice scrupulously finding its way among the apparent complications. It is never fully certain whether he is serious or mocking.

Standing a little back from the mêlée, MADGETT talks to Hardy's mother, a strong-minded woman in her sixties, a contemporary of CISSIE 1, she wears a 'loud' swimming suit and flamboyant sunglasses.

MRS HARDY: This game of yours, Madgett, has everything in it except the kitchen sink.

MADGETT: When played inland, Mrs Hardy, a kitchen sink *is* necessary – here the sea suffices to wash what needs washing.

MRS HARDY: Oh, and what needs washing?

MADGETT: Ask Smut, he's interested in good and evil.

MRS HARDY gives MADGETT a blank look.

Through the mêlée, SMUT is glimpsed on the veranda of CISSIE 2's house. He has a camera around his neck. He is pretending to be a blinded Samson. He gropes his way among the tables and beach chairs to reach two of the wooden pillars that support the veranda roof. He puts his arms around them in the manner of the last action of Samson, grimaces and tries to pull them down. Not surprisingly, he does not succeed. He shrugs, opens his eyes and takes a gherkin off an abandoned food plate, eats it and moves quietly across the veranda to take surreptitious photos of something or somebody we cannot see behind a sheet.

CISSIE 1, leaning on MADGETT's arm as she tips sand out of the sandal.

CISSIE 1: It's too complicated, Madgett.

MADGETT: (*Patiently*) If you are the Hangman, you've got to pair with the Judge over there . . .

CISSIE 1: (*Laughing*) . . . by the time we've learnt your rules it'll be dark.

MADGETT: Anything worth learning takes a little time . . .

69. EXT. THE HOUSE OF CISSIE 2 – VERANDA. DAY
Back of the veranda – at the other end from the tables, BELLAMY and CISSIE 3 are making love on a couch – they are partly hidden by sun awnings and a sheet.
While the camera observes them, SMUT continues his voice-over

which fades up again . . .
SMUT: '. . . the Adulterer can only pair with the Harlot when each has an even number of lives above twelve, though the Dunce can cancel this, provided the Sailor is not batting . . .
(HARDY *bursts in on the newly married couple,* CISSIE 3 *and* BELLAMY.)
HARDY: Come on, you two – out! You can go and do your fornication elsewhere.
CISSIE 3: It's not fornication any more. You buy a marriage licence and it becomes legal.
HARDY: Not on my couch it doesn't. I'll give you three minutes to make yourself decent. Hasn't the novelty worn off yet?
BELLAMY: (*As to an idiot*) Well, you see, Hardy, we've only been married two hours and . . .
HARDY: Like hell – every cow in every field in the district has seen the colour of your arse, Bellamy.
(*He leaves.* BELLAMY *and* CISSIE 3 *are getting back into their swimming costumes.*)
BELLAMY: Crabby idiot! Do you think he ever did it?
CISSIE 3: (*A little sadly*) Ask Cissie.

70. EXT. THE HOUSE OF CISSIE 2 – VERANDA. DAY
A return to the mêlée. Among the montage of action, isolated vignettes of dialogue come through.
NANCY: (*To her brother* GREGORY *who is bowling to* MRS HARDY) Gregory, you're supposed to throw the ball underarm – this isn't Old Trafford.
MRS HARDY: Let him bowl how he likes, I'll still hit it for a six.
(*She does. More explanatory voice-over from* SMUT. *There is no hope of following his complicated explanations.*)
SMUT: . . . the Mother-in-Law is only allotted five runs at a time after which she must defer to the Gravedigger who is allowed to add the number of lives or runs of each competitor he bowls out to his own . . .
MARINA: (*To* MADGETT) Hallo, I'm Bellamy's sister. My name's Marina. Are you Madgett?
MADGETT: I am.
MARINA: If I'm a mourner (*She wears a black veil and hat over a dark bikini*) why do I have to catch one-handed?
MADGETT: Grief is a handicap, Marina. Grief's also blind.

CISSIE 1: (*To* SMUT) What is Sid doing here? (SID *is using his shiny spade to make sandcastles.*)
SMUT: I asked him to come – we might want to bury something.
(*The irritable* HARDY, *caught out in an easy catch, is reluctant to relinquish the bat. Amid jeers he finally throws it down and hurls the hat he is wearing – the Emperor's hat – in the air. A scurry of children chase it.*)
HARDY: He cheated . . . (*Pointing to* TEIGAN, *the bowler;* HARDY *addresses his remarks mainly to his wife,* CISSIE 2.) I do not run a bordello for newlyweds or a pathetic Punch and Judy show for lonely bachelors . . . if the phone rings . . . if someone breaks a leg . . . or if you decide to play a proper game . . . I'm in the sea . . . swimming . . .
(*He strides off angrily.*)
CISSIE 1: What's the matter with him?
CISSIE 2: He's got guts ache – he's always got guts ache.
CISSIE 1: He's always eating. (*In deliberate earshot of* MRS HARDY, *as she,* CISSIE 1, *kneels on the sand painting a red stripe around the knees of small children*) Well, Ophelia, you must have fed him too much sugar when he was a baby.
MRS HARDY: No child of mine had less than he wanted . . .
CISSIE 2: That explains it then.
MRS HARDY: What do you mean?
CISSIE 2: He never learnt to give anything.
BELLAMY: (*Approaching*) Hardy's right. This is my wedding party. Why can't we play some real cricket?
CISSIE 2: Too dangerous.
JONAH: (*Coming up*) What's dangerous about cricket?
MADGETT: The distance you have to walk to the pavilion?
CISSIE 3: There's too much fair play.
MADGETT: And not enough imagination . . . you're not allowed to hit the ball twice and the umpire's not allowed to catch.

71. EXT. THE HOUSE OF CISSIE 2 – BEACH. DAY
While MADGETT is ad-libbing to the aggressive BELLAMY, SMUT and SID, standing side by side, are curiously watching HARDY who seems to be in difficulties with stomach cramps in the water some twenty yards from the shore. SMUT and SID exchange significant looks, but say nothing. MADGETT continues, as NANCY is being eyed up by JONAH and MOSES –

56

who is not at all unaware of their attentions and gauchely reciprocates them.

BELLAMY: What the hell do you know about cricket? It's no more dangerous than any other game.

MADGETT: (*Rising to* BELLAMY's *aggression*) 1931? Chapman Ridger? Australia? A blow on the chest (*He thumps his chest*) . . . hits 51 runs [NUMBER 51] then has heart palpitations for twelve hours – a cracked rib enters the lungs . . . coughing blood, dies the next day in bed with a blonde surfer called Adelaine. . . ? Summer of '52 [NUMBER 52] Hollinghurst at Headingley? A blow to the groin (MADGETT *clutches his groin*)

off-spinner Hoyle . . . reprimanded by the umpire . . . operation, left testicle in a jar in the clubhouse – known as Hollinghurst's Lost Ball . . .
(*As the group of players listen, amused, to* MADGETT, HARDY *in the water is getting into serious difficulties.* SID *and* SMUT, *half watching out of the corner of their eyes, make no move to help.*)
Dendridge at the Oval? Hit on the top of the head (MADGETT *strikes himself a blow and pretends to reel under it – he falls to the sand*) . . . coma . . . his last known words are . . . 'Bugger Bognor' . . . no, sorry, that was Edward VII; sorry, boys, no offence.
CISSIE 2: What's the matter with Madgett – he hates cricket.
MRS HARDY: He's just showing off.
CISSIE 1: He likes acting. (*To* CISSIE 2 *as an aside*) . . . and he might just be distracting everyone from what's happening in the sea.
(CISSIE 2 *turns round to look down the beach to the water.*)
MARINA: What's the matter with Hardy? Does he normally swim so low in the water?

72. EXT. THE HOUSE OF CISSIE 2 – SEA/BEACH. DAY
HARDY in the sea is in pain – his face is contorted – he tries hard to keep afloat. Sensing that others on the beach have seen HARDY's plight, SID and SMUT go into the water to help HARDY

out. JONAH and MOSES and NANCY rush in after them. They bring HARDY out of the sea.
   MRS HARDY: Quick, quick . . . take him inside. Mind his head.
   SMUT: (*Talking to* CISSIE 2 *who stands quietly watching*) Another three minutes, Cissie, and . . . who knows . . . Madgett just ran out of steam . . . I'm sorry.
   CISSIE 2: (*After a pause and without anger*) Smut, you're a little ghoul.

73. INT. THE HOUSE OF CISSIE 2 – SITTING ROOM. DAY
   SMUT: (*Voice over*) The Businessman is never to be trusted. His score is determined by the number of runs scored by his predecessor at the wicket. He is at liberty to change the rules of the game only when he hits a catch. He naturally tries to get players to catch him out.
HARDY is laid on a downstairs couch. He's panting and holding his stomach – but is more aware of having caused a disturbance than anxious about his condition. The rescuers surround him. His mother fusses.
   HARDY: It's all right . . . it's all right, Mother. (*To* CISSIE 2) Get rid of them, Cissie, and find a pair of scissors. I'm all right, Mother . . . leave me alone. I just want to lay still.
   CISSIE 2: Stand aside, Ophelia. You heard what he said.
   (*The game players return to the beach.* HARDY, *reclining on the luridly upholstered couch, naked, fat, vulnerable, with his hair plastered to his forehead – slightly indecent in his vulnerability.* CISSIE 2 *returns with a pair of scissors and a towel and stands over him.*)
   CISSIE 2: Now what?
   HARDY: Cut my hair – I'll feel better.

74. INT. THE HOUSE OF CISSIE 2 – KITCHEN. DAY
SMUT goes to the kitchen fridge and selects an ice lolly. On the inside of the fridge door is a list to be ticked off for ice lollies. The list has reached fifty-three (NUMBER 53). SMUT ticks off his ice lolly.

75. INT. THE HOUSE OF CISSIE 2 – SITTING ROOM. DAY
SMUT returns to the room where HARDY is recovering and watches HARDY and CISSIE 2 through the slightly open door. CISSIE 2 snips at his hair, drying it with a brightly coloured

towel. It is a ritual that CISSIE 2 has grown to know comforts her husband.

CISSIE 2: You eat too much.

HARDY: And you encourage fools too gladly.

SMUT: (*Voice over*) The Businessman can be saved if he submits to a Red Queen – but in doing so, he must pay a forfeit.

76. EXT. THE HOUSE OF CISSIE 2 – BEACH. DAY

SMUT: (*Voice over*) The full flavour of the game of Hangman's Cricket is best appreciated after the game has been played for several hours. By then every player has a fair understanding of the many rules and knows which character he wants to play permanently. Finally an outright loser is found and is obliged to present himself to the Hangman . . . who is always merciless.

A wide shot of the beach. The sun is beginning to set. The game continues on the beach with a few players. Someone has

turned on some music – it is very faint.
In the foreground, SMUT, now with his shirt on, crouches by his bicycle, pumping up the tyre. SID is standing beside him, searching in his waistcoat pocket. He finds several tags and passes them to SMUT.

>   SID: I haven't found fifty-four yet [NUMBER 54].
>   SMUT: (*Taking out a map from his saddle-bag*) It's under a horse-chestnut tree down Nightingale Lane – near a water hydrant.

SMUT gives SID the map which is covered in circles and numbers. SID walks off. SMUT turns on his red bicycle lamp and cycles out of screen, leaving the sun continuing to set over the distant game-players on the beach.

Section 25: The Skipping Girl's House

77. INT./EXT. SKIPPING GIRL'S HOUSE/STREET. NIGHT
Late evening into night. SMUT and the SKIPPING GIRL are sitting just inside the doorway of the SKIPPING GIRL's corridor. Their feet are on the pavement. SMUT's bicycle is propped up against the wall. SMUT has his notepad. The Polaroids he took at the party on the beach are spread out on the step.

>   SMUT: . . . and then Delilah cut off Samson's hair – I think. He was blinded and put in prison. At a large party he summoned up the last of his strength, held on to two pillars and pulled the house down . . . his last words were . . . 'And take good care of Nellie . . .'
>   GIRL: Who was Nellie?
>   SMUT: (*Pointing to a Polaroid on the step*) This is Nellie. Though she sometimes insists on being called Nancy.
>   (*The Polaroid shows* NANCY *in a suggestive clinch with* JONAH *and* MOSES.)
>   GIRL: It was Charles II.
>   SMUT: What was?
>   GIRL: His last words were . . . 'And take good care of Nellie.'
>   SMUT: Who told you that?
>   GIRL: My mother. She says she wishes she'd been Nell Gwyn because she'd like to have serviced Charles II.
>   (*There is a pause while* SMUT *attempts to take this remark in. The* GIRL *gets up to skip – the rope banging on the door jamb.*)

SMUT: You could really come out on to the pavement more – the rope wouldn't slap on the door frame that way.
(*The* GIRL *shakes her head.*)
GIRL: My mother says I'm not to go out. It's dangerous. There are evil men about.

A MAN IN RUNNING SHORTS *runs down the street throwing out coloured streamers from a bag over his shoulder. They watch him pass. He has a vest with 55 on it* (NUMBER 55).

Section 26: Madgett's House

78. INT. MADGETT'S HOUSE – SITTING ROOM. NIGHT
A warm summer night. In the spotlit gloom of rich browns and warm blacks, SMUT, looking vulnerable and white, wearing his reflecting spectacles, stands in his underpants. He is covered in tape crosses, some black, some red, some white – coloured tape familiar from wrapping presents or use in a classroom. They are attached to his arms, his chest, his forehead.
 MADGETT: (*Off-camera*) All right, stand still.
SMUT straightens up and stands still. There is a flash from a camera flash bulb. SMUT looks a vulnerable victim, very innocent.
Wide shot. A view of the whole side of the room. In the foreground, MADGETT sits at a crowded table – open books, charts, old newspapers, a spilled card index. In front of him, an ancient typewriter, pots of ink and ledgers. Further back on the table (covered in a yellowish corded velvet) is a large collection of cricket balls – many of them old, split, 'perished', eaten away, sliced in half – they look like the relics of the orrery of an unknown, grossly debilitated galaxy.
 MADGETT: (*Looking down at his newspaper cuttings*) All right, off-stump crease.
(SMUT *assumes the correct stance at an imaginary cricket crease.*)
Left-handed bat.
(SMUT *changes his bat over to the other side and retakes a position.* MADGETT *gets up from chair and begins to act out the part of a bowler, a new ball in his hand.*)
Right-handed bowler . . . new ball . . . soft ground, off-spinner . . . eeoowweeeeee . . . (MADGETT *brings the ball, still held in his hand, up to a point on* SMUT's *chest.*) . . . splat! (*He looks at newspaper cutting in his left hand.*) . . . No . . . wrong

place . . . too low . . . (*He moves the ball to* SMUT'*s face – to his right eye socket.*) . . . Difficult to see how the ball hit him there . . . still. (MADGETT *reads from newspaper.*) Tolly Schriker. 1931. Made fifty-six runs [NUMBER 56] with one eye closed . . . fell down pavilion steps . . . died in Brisbane Municipal Baths . . . another black cross . . . Stand still.
MADGETT peels off tape from a roll and sticks it above SMUT's right eye, partly masking his sight. He returns to his chair and picks up a Polaroid camera from among a collection of Polaroid photographs and prepares to take a photograph.

79. INT. MADGETT'S HOUSE – SITTING ROOM. NIGHT
SMUT crinkling his forehead under the sticky adhesive tape. There is a flash. CISSIE COLPITTS 3 is in the picture, laden with an armful of long-stemmed cut flowers. She is lit in the momentary flash like a godmother in a dramatic nursery play, with overtones of witchery.
  MADGETT: Smut, pour Cissie a cup of tea.
  CISSIE 1: Don't bother. I'll pour if you're busy playing cricket.
  (*She puts her flowers down on a large armchair, takes off her hat and coat and puts them down on a second chair.*)
  MADGETT: Bellamy has given me the idea for a book of cricketing deaths. Games can be very dangerous.
SMUT moves forward to pour the tea. He pours one for himself and MADGETT and hands them around and sits himself in a large soft armchair in the brown gloom. He looks like a fictional elf – with numbers. The numbers 57, 58, and 59 are stuck on his body (NUMBERS 57, 58 and 59). When he moves, his large shadow moves on the wall. MADGETT, balancing his cup and saucer, finds it difficult to sit down because CISSIE 1's garden produce litters the available chairs.
  CISSIE 1: Madgett, you could speak to Cissie.
  MADGETT: Why could I?
  CISSIE 1: Marrying Bellamy is not the best thing she could have done.
  MADGETT: It's a bit late now.
  CISSIE 1: Why saddle herself with his lechery?
  MADGETT: Are you against lechery?
  CISSIE 1: You know I'm not.
  MADGETT: How do I know that?
  CISSIE 1: (*With a pause and a laugh*) You don't. Lechery is

not fastidious, however, and Bellamy could easily go elsewhere.
MADGETT: Cissie seems to enjoy it.
CISSIE 1: You could make her see reason and she'd thank you for it one day.
MADGETT: Would *he* thank me for it one day? – I don't think so, Cissie. Come on, we're going out. Smut, get your net.
CISSIE 1: Where are we going?
MADGETT: It's a surprise.
SMUT: Do I bring the tea?
MADGETT: No – you do not bring the tea.

Section 27: Madgett's Trysting Field

80. INT./EXT. MADGETT'S CAR/TRYSTING FIELD. NIGHT
A large broad field against a star-lit sky. Madgett's old black car drives slowly across its width in the moonlight, the light beams cutting a swathe in the dark. The car stops in the middle of the field.
SMUT, still with two adhesive crosses on his face, is reading – or attempting to read – in the poor light. He looks out of the back window. CISSIE 1 is in the passenger seat. MADGETT switches on a small orange reading light above the front seats. There is a

figure 60 illuminated on the dashboard (NUMBER 60).
    MADGETT: (*To* SMUT) Try along that hedge.
He points at his own reflection in the windscreen — SMUT looks out of the window, his finger caught in his book where chapter 61 is in evidence (NUMBER 61). SMUT gets out of the car with a collecting net, a torch, a haversack, and three identification books.
SMUT walks across the field away from the car towards the far hedge. He walks along the car headlight beam, his white legs illuminated. The sound of a warm English summer night, an owl, a cock pheasant, crickets, distant sheep.
    CISSIE 1: Well, Madgett, this is nice and quiet and peaceful.
    MADGETT: I thought you'd like it.
    (*There is a long pause. They both listen to the dark field.*)
Well, how are you feeling?
    CISSIE 1: I've never slept better . . . (*Pause, then forthrightly*) Madgett, have you brought me here to claim your reward?
(*She has a wry smile on her face.*)
    MADGETT: Can I kiss you?
    CISSIE 1: (*Smiling*) If you like . . . just here though.
(*She points to her cheek.*)
    MADGETT: That's chaste. Is that all I'm going to get?
    CISSIE 1: Madgett, what do you expect? It's too soon.
    MADGETT: Too soon?
    CISSIE 1: Please believe I appreciate your attentions . . . but, you must wait a little while . . . and who knows . . . your prospects might improve . . . Cissie's more your age. (*She quickly continues, maybe a little too quickly for* MADGETT *looks at her quizzically.*) But don't go getting ideas about Hardy.
MADGETT stares forward out of the windscreen. He turns the headlamps off. There is almost complete darkness in the car. The moon highlights shiny surfaces and suggests the outlines of the two faces staring straight out into the summer evening. Across the field, SMUT's torch and reflecting sheet make a point of light.

81. EXT. TRYSTING FIELD. NIGHT
SMUT in the hedge. The leaves slightly damp. Blackberry leaves, ivy, blackthorn, bracken, cuckoo-pint. SMUT is setting up his moth-sheet under a hawthorn in full blossom. He beats the lower branches of the tree. Petals, twigs and insects rain down. Behind him, 300 yards away, is the MADGETT car with

its orange light on. SMUT's textbook is open at a page of insect illustrations. Two are prominent and marked Figs. 62 and 63 (NUMBERS 62 and 63).

82. INT./EXT. MADGETT'S CAR/TRYSTING FIELD. NIGHT
MADGETT: This time, Cissie, I am not playing games.
CISSIE 1: Aren't you? It's impossible to tell with you. I don't really think you know yourself, do you?
(MADGETT *stares ahead without answering. She follows his gaze.*)
MADGETT: (*After a pause*) I've loved you for years. May I see what I've always wanted to see?
CISSIE 1: What is that?
MADGETT: You without any clothes on.
CISSIE 1: (*Mocking him, but just a trifle anxious*) What a strange desire – now that's a strange game, Madgett.
MADGETT: Is it?
CISSIE 1: . . . Well, here is certainly not the time and place.
(MADGETT *looks sullen.*)
(*Laughing*) Are you going to the police if I don't co-operate?
MADGETT: (*Peevishly*) I might.

83. EXT. HEDGE. NIGHT
Among the petals, twigs and sepals in the sheet, are several fluttering insects, trapped by the light.

84. EXT. TRYSTING FIELD. NIGHT

SMUT's silhouette against the moonlit field, the car is beyond with its orange light. There is a sudden crashing in the undergrowth. Startled, SMUT backs out into the open field, leaving his torch over the moth-collecting sheet.
In his right hand he holds a wriggling, livid-green caterpillar – it's held between his thumb and forefinger – absentmindedly. There is a further crashing and the torch goes out. SMUT runs back across the field to the car.

85. INT./EXT. MADGETT'S CAR/TRYSTING FIELD. NIGHT

In the car, lit by the orange light, CISSIE 1 and MADGETT stare through the windscreen.

    MADGETT: There was a man at Pulham Market who died in his car. He was wealthy – a farmer – he drove his car into a wood near Tomstop – turned off the engine, made himself comfortable and quietly died. I could find absolutely nothing wrong with him . . . (*With a smile*) I expect he died of unrequited love.
    CISSIE 1: Is that what you do if you can't find a cause of death? Write 'died of unrequited love'?
    MADGETT: In his case I wrote 'heart attack after bowls match'.
    CISSIE 1: Trust you to put a game in.

Seen from inside the car, SMUT pushes his face up against the window glass on CISSIE 1's side. The adhesive crosses are still on his face. He has leaves in his hair. CISSIE 1 is only mildly surprised by his presence. SMUT gets in the car. He gets in quietly with a worried face.

    MADGETT: You didn't stay long.
    SMUT: No.
    MADGETT: Where's your torch?
    SMUT: I lost it.
    MADGETT: What do you mean?
    SMUT: I'll come and get it tomorrow.
    CISSIE 1: Did you catch anything interesting?
    SMUT: No.
(SMUT *puts the vivid green caterpillar in* CISSIE 1*'s open palm. It wriggles.* CISSIE 1 *touches* MADGETT*'s arm.*)
    CISSIE 1: Let us go to my place and I'll make some supper.

86. EXT. TRYSTING FIELD. NIGHT
The car travels slowly over the curvature of the field's surface, the starry sky behind, the beam of light shining in the darkness. There is a long line of coloured papers trailing the length of the field – illuminated by the car headlamps. Running mysteriously across the beam, a RUNNER, throwing out coloured papers, disappears into the night. There was a figure 64 on his back (NUMBER 64).

Section 28: Nancy's Bedroom

87. INT. NANCY'S BEDROOM. DAY
NANCY stirring in bed. A noise outside the door. Light streaming in through the window. The situation is identical to the time when CISSIE 3 entered the same bedroom at the same time earlier in the narrative. NANCY sits puzzled and blinking in the sunlight. JAKE's two cousins push open the door and stumble among the shoes scattered on the floor. JONAH, the elder, carries a cup of tea. Without over-emphasis, the scene suggests the story of Susannah and the Elders.
    JONAH: Nancy, good morning, we've made you a cup of tea.
    MOSES: We were impressed by your playing yesterday – you are good at games.
    (NANCY, *puzzled, worried, makes to get out of bed*.)
Don't get out of bed, it must be nice and warm in there. Drink your tea.
    (*The cousins sit down on either side of the bed*.)
    NANCY: I . . . what are you doing here?
    JONAH: Well . . . we've been thinking that . . . you know perhaps more than you've told us.
    NANCY: No.
    JONAH: For instance . . . who's to say that it wasn't you who killed Jake? (*Mock sympathy*) A poor old man of sixty-five [NUMBER 65].
    (NANCY doesn't reply.)
    MOSES: Well? Is silence a confession?
    JONAH: Well, until we know better, Nancy, we'll have to think it was you who . . . drowned him, and I think in the circumstances, that we have a right, being Jake's cousins, to continue . . . where he left off . . .
    MOSES: I think we really ought to work together, don't

you. . . ?
JONAH: Because we've got to trap this crooked coroner.
MOSES: Or . . . or . . . we could go to the police and tell them that you were responsible . . . after all you were the very last person to see him alive . . . weren't you?
JONAH: And the blackmail might as well start now . . . have you finished your tea?
MOSES: Oh . . . just before we start – these shoes all over the place. I don't like women's shoes – so you're going to have to get rid of them.
(*The cousins both slowly slide their hands under the bedsheets.* NANCY *is petrified.*)
JONAH: You're nice and warm.
MOSES: And a little damp in places.
(NANCY *is about to scream.* JONAH, *anticipating it, slams a hand over her mouth.*)

88. EXT. NANCY'S HOUSE – FRONT GARDEN. DAY
The garden is looking bright and attractive in the early morning. After a pause, JONAH, with his shirt unbuttoned, opens the window and begins to throw out handfuls of shoes. They fall into a clump of purple mallow beneath the window. The garden is full of escaped rabbits.

Section 29: The House of Cissie Colpitts 2

89. EXT. THE HOUSE OF CISSIE COLPITTS 2 – VERANDA. DAY
High noon. The monotonous rattle of the typewriter is the only sound heard except for the far away sound of the surf.
HARDY is typing – sitting on the house veranda surrounded by papers and accountancy books. The figure 66 (NUMBER 66) is apparent. Very near his elbow is the remains of lunch – a large midday meal for two. HARDY is wearing a swimming costume, sunglasses and a straw hat – even now, he is eating biscuits and drinking coffee. It's very hot, the sun shining brightly off the white-painted wood and the hot sand, where evidence of the recent wedding party is still apparent. The beach is completely empty.
CISSIE 2, wearing sunglasses and wrapped up in a colourful beachrobe, comes out on to the veranda – she's carrying two ice

lollies – one very red, one very yellow. HARDY doesn't stop typing – doesn't acknowledge her. She nudges him with her foot and gives him the yellow ice lolly. While taking it, he still types with one hand. CISSIE 2 lounges provocatively on the beach sofa. She throws back the beachrobe and has nothing on underneath – the marks of her various swimsuits pattern the bronzed and white spaces of her body. The following dialogue is conducted with great sarcasm.

> CISSIE 2: (*Provocatively*) When you want something, Hardy, how do you ask for it?
> HARDY: (*Still typing*) I say 'please' . . .
> CISSIE 2: Please, Hardy, can we have a fuck?
> HARDY: (*Ignoring her provocation*) . . . or if I'm in the office, I pick up the phone and dial nine.

He continues to type. CISSIE 2 languidly stretches over and picks up the phone from a low table. She dials 9. She has a little trouble with it. She dials again, and again . . . and again. She listens. She smiles when a voice speaks at the other end.
Far off along the beach, in the mirage, runs a MAN. He seems to be running towards the house. He has a bag over his shoulder and seems to be throwing things out of it – it's impossible to see what he is throwing.

> CISSIE 2: (*Holding out the phone to* HARDY *who continues to type*) All I get is the fire brigade or the ambulance or the police . . . which one do you want? Do you want to speak to them?
> HARDY: No, thank you.
> CISSIE 2: (*Into the phone*) I'm sorry . . . there is no fire, burglary, accident . . . rape or . . . murder . . . yet. Thank you. (*She puts down the phone*). But don't go away because we might need you.
> HARDY: (*Just sufficiently amused, and determined to continue to irritate*) I usually find one nine suffices . . . and if it doesn't, then I write a note.
> CISSIE 2: A memorandum? – well – I suppose I could do that.

CISSIE 2 takes a pen and a sheet of paper from HARDY's table and writes a note. The RUNNER along the beach is closer. The distance and the mirage still make his activity ambiguous.
CISSIE 2 hands her note to HARDY who continues to type with one hand. He heavily sucks on his ice lolly while he reads the note.

HARDY: Thank you, dear. (*He reads and smiles.*) And if pressed you know very well that I'll do the best I can to oblige.
CISSIE 2: You are so considerate.
HARDY: And you're so imaginative.
CISSIE 2: Well, I have to be . . . for the two of us.
(*He kneels at the foot of the sofa between her knees, licks his ice lolly and, apparently, for we cannot quite see him do it, he pleasures her with it. She shivers at the cold touch, then enjoys it.*)
Mind the juice doesn't stain the sofa. Show me your tongue. (*He does so.*)
Just as I thought, it's yellow . . .
HARDY: Does that mean I'm unwell?
CISSIE 2: What do you think?
HARDY: A little colouring goes a long way. Artificial colouring can be dangerous.
CISSIE 2: So can too much abstinence.
(HARDY *licks the drips of melting ice from the base of his ice lolly and then puts it back between her legs. She lies back on the sofa slowly sucking at her ice lolly. There is a pause.*)
(*Dropping her sarcastic defence to show a glimmer of real affection*) Now, Hardy . . . I need warming up.
(*She makes to put her arms around his neck – he backs away.*)
My mother says hot tea on a hot day can make a body feel very cool.
HARDY: (*Ignoring her sexual invitation*) Are you about to make some tea? I'm not that thirsty . . . what does your mother say about swimming?
CISSIE 2: (*Re-adopting her sarcastic mood*) Reading between the lines I'd say she'd made at least one public statement about bodies in water. . . ?
HARDY: You Colpitts women obviously have a lot of trouble with men . . . why do you think that is?
CISSIE 2: I'll leave you to think about it.
HARDY: I always think better in the bath . . .
CISSIE 2: I wonder if it was the same with Jake?
(*She smiles.*)
HARDY: (*Picking up a towel*) I don't think Jake was much of a thinking man . . . now I'm going for a swim.
CISSIE 2: (*Stretching provocatively and speaking nonchalantly*) I hope you drown.
HARDY: Thank you.

(*He hands her the remains of his ice lolly.*)
(*With smiling sarcasm before he sets off down the beach*) You can look after my typewriter.
CISSIE 2: Damn your typewriter!
CISSIE 2 hurls the remains of his ice lolly at HARDY's departing back. It misses and falls into the sand – the remaining ice melting fast, the juice being soaked up by the sand.

90. EXT. THE HOUSE OF CISSIE COLPITTS 2 – BEACH. DAY
HARDY walks down the beach to the sea. The RUNNER throwing out paper streamers for the paperchase runs across the strip of beach just in front of HARDY. HARDY steps over the trail of papers, steps out of his beach shoes. Some of the red papers cling for a moment to his heel. He walks into the sea.

91. EXT. THE HOUSE OF CISSIE COLPITTS 2 – VERANDA. DAY
On the veranda, CISSIE 2 picks up a lemonade bottle and pours its contents on the typewriter keys, the lemonade gurgles out of the bottle and splashes among the keys.
She picks up a pair of binoculars and watches first the departing RUNNER and then HARDY. She swings the binoculars round to look up the beach the other way. Far off, at the end of the lens, run a little group of runners, jogging in the heat. She swings the binoculars back to HARDY – he is in trouble in the water – waving a hand in the air and making an inordinate amount of splashing.
CISSIE 2: Stupid, bloody idiot.
She stands up and puts on a bathing suit. She picks up a bucket of fine dry sand and pours it over the typewriter keys – the sand fills the body of the machine, sticking to the lemonade-soaked parts. She experimentally pushes a key – the letter h – it makes a graunching sound – the key face never reaches the paper. She types out the number 67 . . . the 7 barely types . . . she tries 68 . . . the 8 barely types . . . she tries 69 . . . it types (NUMBERS 67, 68 and 69). She tries to type out HARDY's name in capitals . . . it gets as far as 'Hard' and then will not type any more.

92. EXT. SEA/BEACH. DAY
In the sea, HARDY, blue in the face and beginning to panic, struggles in the waves.
CISSIE 2 nonchalantly walks down the beach. The runners in the distance are a little nearer. She wades into the sea and swims

close to Hardy.
CISSIE 2: What's the matter?
HARDY: My stomach.
CISSIE 2: What of your stomach? No one can see it here – for a change.
HARDY: Don't fool around – get me out.
CISSIE 2: I've just ruined your very best typewriter.
HARDY: You've what?
CISSIE 2: And now I'm going to do my best to drown you.
HARDY: The Colpitts prerogative.
(*Grabbing him from behind, she pulls him under – he splutters and curses and tries to cry for help. The runners are closer.*)
CISSIE 2: You're so stubborn – you won't sink.
(*She tries to pull him under again.*)
HARDY: All right – for God's sake – Cissie, get me out.
CISSIE 2: Do you think I can pull it off?
HARDY: Pull what off?
CISSIE 2: Your drowning, you dope.
HARDY: You haven't a chance . . .
(CISSIE 2 *pulls him under, splashing to prevent him shouting.*)
CISSIE 2: All right – that was a preliminary – here comes the real attempt. One –
(*She pulls him under and keeps him there – finally releasing him, he comes up spluttering and struggling.*)
My word, Hardy, it must be your belly that keeps you afloat. You and your belly are stubborn.
HARDY: Cissie – please – I can't move my legs – I'm in pain.
CISSIE 2: I've been in pain a long time. (*She ducks him again.*) Two . . .
(*The waves continue to strike the shore, the seagulls wheel.*)
Three.
HARDY: It's no good, Cissie, you'll have to try harder.
CISSIE 2: Three times, Hardy, isn't that enough? Because that's the allotted number. (*She shouts in his ear.*) Is that enough, you big fat dope?
He sinks. CISSIE 2 waits patiently, squeezing the water from her ear. HARDY's body rises.
CISSIE 2 lets a distance come between herself and HARDY – then, satisfying herself that it is likely no one saw her – and with a loudness that surprises herself – she sets up a shouting and screaming – directed at the runners that have now come abreast the beach, following the scattered paper trail.

93. EXT. THE HOUSE OF CISSIE COLPITTS 2 – BEACH. DAY
The runners break their formation – some are nearly naked, running in the heat. All are hot and sweating. They behave like curious animals – standing, panting, waiting, wading into the surf – they have the sort of motivation expected of idle cows. Two of them, oblivious to the drama, start a game of leapfrog. Two of the runners with the numbers 70 and 71 drag HARDY out of the sea. Then the others help. HARDY is laid on the beach. They pump his arms and beat his chest – all without talking, and with several curious and appraising glances at CISSIE 2. The runners – some five or six of them try mouth-to-mouth resuscitation. They spit out sea water from HARDY's lungs. Finally CISSIE 2 kneels down to give HARDY the kiss of life. She hesitates making lip contact – HARDY's mouth is covered in spittle – most of it not of his making. She finally kisses him on the forehead. She walks up the beach, the runners carrying HARDY behind her.

94. INT./EXT. THE HOUSE OF CISSIE COLPITTS 2 – VERANDA/SITTING ROOM. DAY
Looking towards the open door, the runners stand about, sit on the veranda steps, peer through the window – beyond them the sand and the sky.
  CISSIE 2: Leave me now – I want to be alone with him.
  RUNNER: (*With sympathy*) We can't leave you.
  CISSIE 2: (*A little sharply*) Yes, you can – he's my husband.
  RUNNER: Where's your phone?
  CISSIE 2: It's all right . . . you must let me phone the police . . . or the ambulance . . . (*Absent-mindedly*) . . . or the fire brigade . . . and . . . the coroner.
  RUNNER: Are you sure you're going to be all right? If you want a witness – our name is Van Dyke.
  CISSIE 2: All right, thank you. (*She smiles, reading off their numbered vests.*) Mr 70 and Mr 71 Van Dyke [NUMBERS 70 and 71].
CISSIE 2 nods her head. While the other runners mooch about like curious cows, NUMBERS 70 and 71 hover, expecting to do more. CISSIE 2 smoothes HARDY's wet hair off his face. A runner scratches his back on a wooden moulding of the veranda. The runners leave the house, walking backwards. CISSIE 2 takes a pair of scissors and begins to cut HARDY's hair. After a moment's hesitation, she starts to cut his beard close to his face.

His head is cradled in her lap.
The runners move away. Some of them run backwards a little way, or run on the spot on the soft sand. CISSIE 2 picks up the phone and slowly dials a number and the last runner moves off to join the straggling crocodile of runners that stretches down to the beach and the water margin. The seagulls leave with them. Before she has finished dialling, she puts down the phone, takes up a razor and carefully shaves HARDY.

Section 30: Madgett's House

95. INT. MADGETT'S HOUSE – SITTING ROOM. DAY
The sun streaming into the room from the left-hand side. Fastened to the back wall are three identical and enlarged life-size line drawings of W. G. Grace, the cricketer. On each of them – more complicated than a star map – are numerous figures, numbers and crosses.
SMUT, in short trousers and with a pencil behind his ear, and with grubby, ink-stained fingers, is working on the second and middle drawing, writing further details on to the paper with a meticulous hand. As reference, he uses a clutch of Polaroid photographs, held fan-wise in his left hand – the Polaroids are of himself covered in adhesive-coloured crosses.
There is a figure 72 scrawled across one of them (NUMBER 72). SMUT's dog, in dishevelled curlers and snatches of bright ribbon, is chewing a bone on the carpet. MADGETT, carrying a bowl of chocolate pudding, enters. He is dressed in a worn dressing-gown.
He is carrying a handful of postcards and letters. He reads distastefully.
> MADGETT: '. . . grown men don't die in their baths without a little help, perhaps from their wives. . . ?' (*He reads a second letter.*) '. . . those three Colpitts women are witches, Madgett, let's hope you can swim!' – Well, every good game ought to have its barracking.

MADGETT throws the postcards and letters down on the table. He sits down in front of his typewriter. He stares at the sheet in the typewriter: 'Statistical report on Cricketing Accidents, 1694–1982' by Henry Madgett. He spoons chocolate pudding into his mouth. The phone rings right by his arm.

CISSIE 2: Madgett? Hello.
MADGETT: Cissie? Hello.

96. INT. THE HOUSE OF CISSIE COLPITTS 2 – SITTING ROOM. DAY
Cut to CISSIE 2 making the call. She is seated on the floor, leaning back on the couch where HARDY is lying. His left hand is trailing down the side of the couch – his white skin showing brightly against the livid red and maroon of the couch. CISSIE 2's head obscures the fact that he is wearing swimming trunks. The shaving things are neatly arranged on the carpet. She is very calm.
CISSIE 2: Madgett, I think you've got to come at once.
MADGETT: But I'm in the bath.
CISSIE 2: I didn't know you had a phone in the bathroom. Have you remembered to turn the tap off? Water's dangerous.
MADGETT: Hot water?
CISSIE 2: Yes, hot water – figuratively speaking.
MADGETT: You never were one for figures of speech – something is obviously wrong.
CISSIE 2: Or right?

97. INT. MADGETT'S HOUSE – SITTING ROOM. DAY
Cut to MADGETT. He looks weary.
MADGETT: Cissie, do you need the services of a coroner . . . or an admirer?
CISSIE 2: Both.
MADGETT: (*After a pause*) What's in it for me? I need a lasting reward.
CISSIE 2: Madgett, are you blackmailing me?
MADGETT: (*Resignedly*) Cissie, consider what I'm staking on your matrimonial games.
CISSIE 2: This particular matrimonial game is finished.
MADGETT: Do you intend starting a new one?

98. THE HOUSE OF CISSIE COLPITTS 2 – SITTING ROOM. DAY
Cut to CISSIE 2.
CISSIE 2: With whom . . . (*A pause.*) I would have thought you had enough games going to last you a life time . . . (*There's another pause.*) You helped my mother. I felt sure

you'd help me . . . that's all. (*A pause*.) You haven't really got a phone in the bathroom, have you?
MADGETT: You're right.
CISSIE 2: So why say you have?

99. INT. MADGETT'S HOUSE – SITTING ROOM. DAY
Cut to MADGETT – he is facing the camera, possibly to direct his speech away from SMUT, who is taking the beards off the figure outlines of W. G. Grace.
MADGETT: I can cope with bad news in a bathroom – perhaps it's the echo or the warmth.
CISSIE 2: Good Lord – that's what Hardy said.
MADGETT: His last words?
CISSIE 2: No.
MADGETT: What were his last words? 'Kiss me, Nelson'?
CISSIE 2: No. 'You'll have to try harder.'

Section 31: The Jetty

100. EXT. NANCY'S JETTY. DAY
Against a large open sky, NANCY tearfully wheels a wheelbarrow of shoes down a long slatted wooden jetty to the edge of the river. She hesitates and then tips the shoes into the water. She stands with the empty barrow with the tears streaming down her face. Thwarted gulls, expecting food, dip and dive over the shoes – some sink, some momentarily float. Finally, they all sink.

Section 32: The House of Cissie Colpitts 2

101. INT. THE HOUSE OF CISSIE COLPITTS 2 – SITTING ROOM. DAY
The three CISSIES surround HARDY's body on the couch. CISSIE 1 sweeps up the hair shavings. CISSIE 2 is washing his feet, and getting the sand out from between his toes. The 'arranged' tableau is vaguely reminiscent of a Deposition from the Cross.
CISSIE 3: It's surprising – do all fat men have little willies?
CISSIE 1: God – I wonder how many women have asked him that?

CISSIE 2: (*Looking at her mother*) Not many – they seem to ask me instead.
CISSIE 3: And what do you answer?
CISSIE 2: In this case I'd say it was the effect of cold water.
CISSIE 3: Do they shrink at death?
(*Behind her,* MADGETT *and* SMUT *are seen coming across the beach and into the house through the veranda entrance.*)
CISSIE 2: Why don't you ask Bellamy?
CISSIE 1: Why don't you ask Madgett – he's a medical man.
(MADGETT *and* SMUT *enter the room.* MADGETT *pauses and eyes each woman in turn – they stare silently back at him.* MADGETT *shivers.*)
MADGETT: It's cold in here – Smut, go and make a cup of tea.
(*After* SMUT *has left the room –*)
You women are getting too proficient at this.
CISSIE 2: (*With the slightest of smiles*) We aim to please the coroner . . .
CISSIE 1: The body is already undressed.
MADGETT: I did not imagine he went swimming with his clothes on.
CISSIE 1: Doesn't it make it easier for you?
MADGETT: Nothing you do makes it easier for me. You've got to stop. (*Very unemotionally*) One is just possible, two is very unlikely . . . you have no prerogative on drowning. The coroner's office is inviolate.
CISSIE 3: What?
MADGETT: Not violate.
CISSIE 1: (*With affectionate sarcasm*) Of course it's not.
CISSIE 2: Don't be so melodramatic, Madgett.
MADGETT: I feel ill.
CISSIE 1: Why do you always feel ill at times like this?
MADGETT: It's the excitement – it goes to my stomach.
CISSIE 3: I'd have thought you would have got over that by now.
MADGETT: (*Wearily*) It's only with special cases.
CISSIE 2: What special cases?
CISSIE 1: (*Sympathetically*) Drownings?
MADGETT: Yes . . . and women.
CISSIE 3: Women?
MADGETT: Yes . . . and personal involvements.
CISSIE 2: Haven't you heard of coincidence?

MADGETT: I've heard of it.
CISSIE 2: Doesn't it appeal to you?
MADGETT: Only as an idea – not as a policy inquiry.
(SMUT *comes in with the tea.*)
SMUT: Cissie, where did it happen?
CISSIE 2: On the beach.
SMUT: Could you say exactly where on the beach?
CISSIE 2: It's now covered with the tide. (*She looks out of the window.*) Smut, have you brought your red paint?
SMUT: (*Very seriously*) No, Cissie, today is Tuesday. Tuesday's colour is yellow.
CISSIE 2: (*Completely upstaged*) Oh.
MADGETT: (*Testing the temperature of the body*) I'm bound to say that . . . I could try and revive him even now . . . it has been known . . .
CISSIE 2: Don't be stupid, Madgett . . . and don't try. The man's name is Hardy not Lazarus.

CISSIE 2, who has been sweeping up the hair and beard clippings very carefully from the carpet and the couch, mounds them up on a newspaper. She picks up a largish flower pot, lifts out the geranium with its roots, puts HARDY's hair in the pot and puts back the plant. She is watched in curious fascination by everyone else.

CISSIE 2: (*Looking up at their wondering eyes*) Just being tidy.

102. THE HOUSE OF CISSIE COLPITTS 2 – VERANDA. DAY
Outside on the veranda, SID THE DIGGER waits with his shiny spade. Behind him is Madgett's car with the doors open. Behind again, walking across the distant beach, pushing a wheelbarrow, is NANCY. She looks curiously in the direction of the house.

Section 33: Crematorium 2

103. EXT. CREMATORIUM 2. DAY
At a second crematorium – different from the first one where Jake was cremated. In the background is the crematorium chimney. The ceremony is over and the mourners are walking down a wide path towards the camera. MADGETT and CISSIE 2 are walking between CISSIE 1 and CISSIE 3. Behind them, among the other mourners is MRS HARDY (CISSIE 2'S MOTHER-IN-LAW), the two RUNNERS from the beach,

JAKE's cousins and NANCY.
CISSIE 2 is weeping – quite genuinely. They walk past a gravestone marked with an inscription that discreetly reads '. . . aged 73' (NUMBER 73).
> MADGETT: I shouldn't concern yourself too much – a great many things are dying very violently all the time – ask Smut.
> CISSIE 2: Small comfort, Madgett.
> MADGETT: On the contrary, I'd say great relief.
> CISSIE 2: I'd rather be alive and alone than dead in company.

Behind MADGETT and CISSIE 2 is MRS HARDY walking between the two RUNNERS from the beach – they tower over her, and are in urgent unheard conversation with her.
CISSIE 2 suddenly stops dead and there is a tendency for the informal procession to ricochet into her. CISSIE 2 puts her hands to her ears.
> MADGETT: What are you doing that for?
> CISSIE 2: Smut has just got into your car . . . he quite liked Hardy . . . and there's been a robbery at the fireworks factory.

On CISSIE 2's last word, a barrage of rockets roars up into the daytime sky. Dogs bark.
A two-shot of MADGETT and CISSIE 2 – CISSIE 2 with a tear-stained face and MADGETT looking white and lugubrious – lit by the dramatic changing light of daytime fireworks. SMUT, pressing his nose to the car window, watches, his face partly obliterated by the fireworks' reflection.
A sudden shouting breaks out as MOSES BOGNOR, one of JAKE's cousins, catches fire – his jacket is smoking and smouldering. JONAH and GREGORY douse him with a convenient cemetery bucket of water. He is soaked. He is standing by a grave marked with a 74 (NUMBER 74).

Section 34: *Madgett's Car*

104. INT./EXT. MADGETT'S CAR/WATER TOWER 2. DAY
MADGETT, SMUT and the COLPITTS WOMEN are driving home from the funeral. A water tower looms on the horizon – a different one from before.
> MADGETT: (*Laughing*) There's a water tower coming up.
> SMUT: We don't go near it, we take the left turning.
> CISSIE 3: What a pity.

CISSIE 2: Turn right – go on, turn right.
MADGETT: But it's out of our way.
CISSIE 2: No matter – you didn't exactly hurry us there, so why hurry us back?
CISSIE 1: I like water towers . . . and what's the betting . . . ?
(*They've turned right and under the tower and alongside it are parked six cars and a little knot of people talking.*)
. . . and what's the betting that the water tower conspirators are convening . . . ?
CISSIE 3: Hail Mary! Bloody hell, Madgett!
SMUT: Cissie!
CISSIE 3: Sorry, Smut.
CISSIE 2: There they are. Hardy's mother, Jake's cousins . . .
CISSIE 3: And Nancy. She's been very haunted-looking recently.
CISSIE 2: God! There's those two runners from the beach.
CISSIE 3: What are they planning now?
MADGETT: It's one conspiracy against another. Yours against theirs. Yours to drown, theirs to prosecute.
CISSIE 2: Hardy's mother would prosecute her milkman for leaving three pints instead of two.
(SPLASH BELLAMY *appears in the group – he's previously been obscured by the others, holding back, a little shame-faced.*)
CISSIE 3: Bloody hell – Splash is there – he hates funerals. I'm going to find out what he's doing.
CISSIE 1: Don't do that. Drive on, Madgett, we don't want to get mixed up in arguments with all that water over our heads. That's asking for trouble.

Section 35: Skipping Girl's House

105. EXT. SKIPPING GIRL'S HOUSE. EVENING
Evening – an orange glow lights up the front of the SKIPPING GIRL's house. SMUT in his funeral clothes – long trousers and white shirt with a frayed collar – sits on the steps of the house. She is a little more elaborately dressed than she was before – more ribbons, more bows. She skips a little forward of her doorstep – sufficient for SMUT to be seated behind her. He is putting out Polaroid photos on the step – photos of the cricket game that was played at BELLAMY's wedding party.

The photos show a more profligate party than seemed to be the case.
There is conversation up above in the upper rooms of the house. It is unintelligible but sounds angry.

>   SMUT: . . . then this woman tipped a bucket of sand and a bottle of lemonade over his typewriter. He went for a swim in the sea and because he had eaten too much he got stomach cramps . . . and drowned. Seven men gave him the kiss of life, but it didn't work. She knew it wouldn't. She cut all his hair off with a pair of blunt scissors . . . just like Delilah . . . this game is called Hangman's Cricket . . .

As he speaks there is a bustling in the corridor behind him – two POLICEMEN – one of them who was present at JAKE's removal from the bath and who acts as a police coroner – come down the corridor and out on to the step.
One of the POLICEMEN speaks to SMUT.

>   POLICEMAN: What's that about hangmen?
>   SMUT: It's a game of cricket . . . you really need seventy-five players [NUMBER 75] . . . six sides of twelve and three umpires.
>   (*The* POLICEMAN *picks up a photo and examines it – it's a suggestive Polaroid of* NANCY *and* JAKE's *two cousins.*)
>   POLICEMAN: Have you any more of these?
>   SMUT: Hundreds.

POLICEMAN: Where do they come from?
SMUT: I've taken them.
POLICEMAN: You've taken them – I don't believe you.
(SMUT *shrugs and holds his hand out for the photo. The* POLICEMAN *gives it to him, then both policemen turn slowly away and walk off down the street.*)
SMUT: What was all that about?
GIRL: Oh, nothing – they're friends of my mother's. I'm going to another party tonight.
SMUT: (*Enviously*) Where?
GIRL: (*Casually*) A dance hall overlooking the sea . . . with lights, where we are going to eat crab paste and sprats in batter and be sick in airline bags. We're each going to be given a black rabbit as a going-home present.
SMUT: (*Trying not to show his envy*) Oh? If you skipped a little further out you could swing the rope harder. Have you heard the story about Potiphar's wife?
GIRL: No – who's she?
SMUT: She was like your mother.
GIRL: Oh? My mother's never been married.
SMUT: Oh.

Section 36: Cissie Colpitts 3 and Bellamy's Bicycle Ride

106. EXT. COUNTRY LANE. DAY
An uphill sunlit country lane. Mid-afternoon. CISSIE 3 and BELLAMY are cycling up the hill, standing on the pedals. They talk between breaths. Along one side of the lane, the paper-chaser has left a trail of streamers – light blue, dark blue, black and white tissue paper.
CISSIE 3: (*Teasingly inquiring*) How is it that a non-swimmer belongs to a water-tower conspiracy, Bellamy?
BELLAMY: What?
CISSIE 3: A water-tower conspiracy.
BELLAMY: (*Disingenuously*) You've noticed?
CISSIE 3: (*Exasperated*) Come on!
BELLAMY: It's just a convenient place to meet.
CISSIE 3: Is there is a subscription list?
BELLAMY: (*Dubiously*) Yes.

CISSIE 3: (*Ridiculing him*) And a secret sign? A flying fish? Or wear something black and blue – death by water – the colour of bruising?
(BELLAMY *answers with a scornful look. They've reached the top of the hill and begin to glide down the other side. The trees flick past faster and faster.*)
And how long is your subscription list?
BELLAMY: Long enough.
CISSIE 3: Oh?
BELLAMY: Yes – all those who think the Colpitts deaths are not accidental.
CISSIE 3: (*Disparagingly*) I guessed that much. (*She now has to raise her voice to be heard above the slipstream.*) And what do you intend doing about it?
BELLAMY: (*Shouting*) For a start – get Madgett investigated.
CISSIE 3: (*Shouting*) That sounds business-like . . . are you going to alert the Water Board?
(*She laughs, holding her head back so that the slipstream flies into her mouth.*)
They cycle round a bend very fast and momentarily are lost to view – there is the sound of a crash and a scream.
They have both crashed into two dead black-and-white cows strewn across the corner of the country lane. Flies buzz. Maybe the cows are victims of a traffic accident. Each cow has a number stencilled across its rump – numbers 76 and 77 (NUMBERS 76 and 77). CISSIE 3 has gashed her hip – she pulls down her shorts to examine the bruise. BELLAMY has been thrown into a messy mêlée of spilled intestines and blood. There are heavy skid marks on the road. The paper trail stops dead at the corpses.
CISSIE 3: God – poor cows.
(*She sniffs the air.* BELLAMY *extricates himself, his hands covered in gore. He wipes them on the cow's hide, then sniffs his fingers.*)
BELLAMY: Bloody hell, this isn't all blood – it's red paint, that little ghoul has been here already.
(*Another view reveals* SMUT'S *careful, methodical clerkmanship by the numbers and crosses painted on the road – numbers 78 and 79* (NUMBERS 78 and 79) *and an identifying red-painted stake planted in the verge.*)
CISSIE 3: (*Sniffing*) I thought I could smell gunpowder.
BELLAMY: I thought it was the sickly smell of death.

CISSIE 3: It's too early for that . . . yet . . . (*She smiles.*)
Bellamy, this conspiracy of yours . . . do you regard me as an accessory? Because if I am, I'd better get rid of you quick.
BELLAMY: I'd like to see you try.
CISSIE 3: (*Musing and smiling*) I don't think you're allowed to screw your wife in prison . . . so I suggest that – just in case you are seriously working on it – we'd better make good use of my free time now. Kiss my backside.
(*She takes down her shorts and lies on the road on her stomach.*)
BELLAMY: (*Disturbed and disquieted*) No. Not here, you fool!
CISSIE 3: Why not?
(*She looks at him quizzically.*)
The camera cranes up above the hedge. On the field on the other side, SID THE DIGGER is approaching with his shining spade over his shoulder. BELLAMY kisses CISSIE 3's backside.

Section 37: *Madgett's Trysting Field*

107. INT./EXT. MADGETT'S CAR/TRYSTING FIELD. DUSK
In Madgett's car driving over the field – the sun is setting in the background, the long shadows from the surrounding hedges throw the individual grass stems into relief. CISSIE 2 and MADGETT are in the car. There is music on the car radio.
CISSIE 2: Madgett, this is a bit irresponsible, isn't it?
MADGETT: What is?
CISSIE 2: Driving over the grass like this.
MADGETT: Oh, it's sheep pasture . . . and the sheep won't mind.
The car slows to a halt. MADGETT turns off the engine. The music – an elegiac, funereal, melancholic, orchestral piece continues to play on the car radio.
MADGETT: Right, Smut, try the alders.
SMUT is sitting in the back seat apparently poring over his insect book where a page of illustrations reveals Fig. 80 and Fig. 81 (NUMBERS 80 and 81). All three get out of the car. CISSIE 2 sits on the bonnet. MADGETT fidgets. SMUT sets off for the hedge with his equipment, the two adults watching him go. An evening breeze blows in CISSIE 2's hair.
MADGETT: (*With studied indifference*) All right, Cissie. Will you marry me?
CISSIE 2: No, Madgett, I could never marry a coroner. I

could never be sure that you'd washed your hands. (*Laughing*) Besides, how could I trust a game-player?

MADGETT: I'm not playing games at this particular time. (*He looks glum and serious.*)

CISSIE 2: You're far more entertaining when you *are*, Madgett.

(*A prolonged silence from* MADGETT.)

Besides, you are far more valuable to me as a friend . . . (*She baits him*) As a coroner?

MADGETT: (*After a pause*) How about . . . as a lover?

CISSIE 2: (*With affection and touching his arm*) Well, Madgett . . . I *admit* to drowning Hardy . . . possibly for *not* being a satisfactory lover . . . (*She laughs*) . . . and give or take an inch, you could get into his trousers, but I don't think I drowned him so that you could make use of his bed. (*She changes the subject.*) Cissie's looking for a father figure . . . (MADGETT *looks quizzically at her.*)

. . . but as much as I dislike Bellamy, don't go getting ideas – remember you're a coroner.

MADGETT: (*Lugubriously*) All coroners see is corpses.

CISSIE 2: (*Laughing and with a touch of spite*) Well . . . they won't reject you . . . tell me, Madgett, have you ever fallen in love with one of your corpses?

It's now grown dark and CISSIE 2 and MADGETT walk slowly down towards where SMUT should be collecting insects. The breeze blows the grass. CISSIE 2 reaches out and links her arm with MADGETT's. The music on the car radio continues very faintly – growing more faint all the time until it is lost in the soft mists of the night field.

MADGETT: Yes . . . several . . .

CISSIE 2: And did you ever . . . do anything?

MADGETT: (*Smiling sadly*) Yes. I kissed an old lady of eighty-two once . . . on the forehead [NUMBER 82]. She was twice my age.

CISSIE 2: Is that all? Was she the only one?

MADGETT: No . . . she wasn't, but I'm not going to say any more.

CISSIE 2: Really, Madgett. (*Reprovingly*) Tell me.

MADGETT: Well . . . I once sat up all night with a girl who'd been run down by cows. There wasn't a mark on her, but her skull was fractured. She was nineteen. She had fair hair and blue eyes [*A description of* CISSIE 3].

CISSIE 2: If she was dead, how could you see the colour of her eyes?
MADGETT: That was the problem. I couldn't bring myself to close them . . . they were beautiful.
CISSIE 2: (*Egging him on*) So what did you do?
MADGETT: I sat beside her . . . and held her hand . . . and I'm not saying any more . . . but I wasn't invited to the funeral.
CISSIE 2: Well, I'll tell you what, you can come to mine – I'm inviting you now, and, I don't mind – on the whole – if you take liberties . . . (*Laughing*) as long as they're not too gross . . . in fact, if I was *very* old, I'm sure I'd be flattered.
MADGETT: I would prefer to be encouraged to take liberties now.
CISSIE 2: Well, I certainly don't feel like it at this moment.
MADGETT: Look, Cissie, (*With some exasperation*) I have a reputation at stake – thanks to you and your mother . . . and I'm sure Smut will not want a father who's an accomplice to murder.
CISSIE 2: Come on, Madgett! It was his idea!
MADGETT: *His* idea!
CISSIE 2: Well, not quite, but I acted on something he said. He understands.
MADGETT: Understands what?
CISSIE 2: That . . . (*With a laugh*) coroners need corpses . . . (*Laughing more loudly*) like gravediggers need corpses. You notice how Sid follows him around like a black shadow?
MADGETT: Sid's known him since he was a baby.

108. EXT. TRYSTING FIELD. DUSK
MADGETT and CISSIE 2 have both come up to the spot in the hedge where they supposed SMUT would be. His torch – still alight – is propped up above the white collecting sheet he's put out. But he's not there. MADGETT and CISSIE 2 are illuminated in the torchlight with a background of the last of the twilight and the beams of the car headlights at the top of the field behind them. The field is full of twilight noises – low birdsong, a distant owl, a breeze.
CISSIE 2: You know Smut is devoted to you.
MADGETT: Enough to know how devoted I am to you?
CISSIE 2: (*Genuinely surprised*) There's a thought. Would he

have acted on it? He's certainly going to be very interesting when he grows up.
MADGETT: I've noticed how you're all so fond of kissing him.
CISSIE 2: Where's he gone?
(*They both call him – first softly, then more loudly. There is nothing except the twilight noises and the slightest rustling in the hedge.*)
MADGETT: It's all right – he's probably sloped off home. (*He eats a blackberry from the hedge.*) We must go blackberrying. You could come with us.
CISSIE 2: No, thank you. Smut'll need to count them and his counting drives me up the wall.

Section 38: Madgett's House

109. INT. MADGETT'S HOUSE – SMUT'S BEDROOM. NIGHT
Interior of SMUT's bedroom looking towards the window, the car headlights illuminate the eggs suspended from the ceiling and the model of 200 sheep grouped on an imitation field. The headlights project a shadow of the number 83 on the wall.
(NUMBER 83). The sound of the engine is heard to switch off, car doors slam, the car radio is switched off and the headlamps switched off.
CISSIE 2: (*Distant call from the garden*) Smut. Smut – are you in?
MADGETT: There's a light on in the bedroom – he's probably asleep.
The camera makes a 180 degree pan, slowly revealing SMUT's bedroom, his models, books, pictures, his long line of table lamps. The last table lamp, nearest his bed, is on. Its light illuminates SMUT. He's sitting up – bolt upright – in his large double bed. A large bed for one so small. He is bravely clutching a book and a glass of pink gargle water. The large white sheet that covers him and his bed is blood-stained around his groin – a large circular red stain. MADGETT and CISSIE 2, who we have heard all this time coming up the stairs, enter the room. MADGETT stares at SMUT.
MADGETT: God . . . Smut? . . . he's circumcised himself . . . get a doctor . . . call a doctor . . . I can't look.
(CISSIE 2 *looks under the sheet,* SMUT *all the while gritting his teeth.*)

CISSIE 2: Smut . . . (*She shakes him.*) Smut – what did you do it with?
SMUT: It's all right, Cissie, I sterilized the scissors.
CISSIE 2: The scissors?

Section 39: Swimming Pool – Cissie Colpitts 3's and Bellamy's Swimming Lesson

110. INT. SWIMMING POOL. DAY
On a hot afternoon in a late-Victorian swimming pool. A municipal swimming pool. At about two in the afternoon. Bright white light streaming from a glassed roof. So bright that it's difficult to look up at the glass. The light streams down on to the water like lights over a pool table. Numbered rows of battered wooden cubicles around the edges of the bath. The numbers are stencilled on with an unfashionable template – a reddish brown on duck-shell turquoise. A brass tap, polished to the detriment of the cream-painted wall behind it, drips into a shallow and yellow-tiled footbath. A cricket commentary on a transistor radio drones relentlessly, its exact sense lost in the echoic spaces of the pool. The figure 84 (NUMBER 84) is noticeable on a cubicle door, the only door that is open.
CISSIE 3 is giving BELLAMY a swimming lesson. He is in the water with floats. He looks white and a little scared. CISSIE 3, in a bright-red swimming costume that hugs her body, swims beside him. Her hair floats in the water. She holds his feet and exhorts him to strike out with his arms. She deliberately tips him forward so that he splutters with a mouthful of water. He blusters and shouts at her. She laughs and, swimming lazily on her back, moves around him. He strikes out at her, moving all the time into deeper water. She catches his hand and draws herself towards him.
CISSIE 3: You've got to stop striking about like a stranded fish. Use your legs.
BELLAMY: You're just here to make fun of me. I'm giving up.
CISSIE 3: Don't be stupid. Let's try a length. Take your floats off.
BELLAMY: No. I'm not ready yet.
CISSIE 3: Yes, you are. Come here.

(CISSIE 3 *holds his head and kisses him. He responds despite the insecurity of his position. Only just treading the pool bottom, he grasps her body.*)
Don't, someone might come in.
BELLAMY: You said we had the place to ourselves. That was what we agreed on.
CISSIE 3: Frightened of being seen wallowing in the water like a baby?
BELLAMY: Come here.
(*He makes to kiss her again, she responds, treading water he slips her costume off her shoulders.*)
CISSIE 3: You *are* getting more confident in water. (*She slides her hand into his costume.*) Take your costume off.
(*He looks around the pool edge and towards the doors.*)
It's all right, I've locked the doors. Here's the key, look.
Around her neck is a large key on a string, along with the cubicle key. The key is numbered 85 (NUMBER 85).
The white light shines brightly down on the figures in the water. The reflections flashing and breaking, the blue lines on the pool bottom distorting and reflecting. The two bodies seen from above and beneath the water, interrupted visually by bubbles and water movement. She slips his costume to his ankles, allowing him to manoeuvre her costume down to her hips. Then, in a last and truly affectionate embrace, kisses him on the mouth, paddling him into deeper water, her left hand between his legs to distract him, her right hand searching for the strings that attach the floats to his upper arms. She pulls the strings and the floats float away. Slowly she breaks from him and, gently moving her limbs, paddles backwards, making deceptive moves to take off her costume. But she doesn't. For several seconds BELLAMY hasn't realized what is going on. By the time CISSIE 3 is four yards from him and too far for him to reach, he is floundering. He begins to panic, the costume around his ankles severely hampering him.
CISSIE 3 swims to the pool edge. She climbs out, holding on to the key around her neck; she stands on the pool edge making no attempt to cover the upper part of her body with the costume. He sees her standing on the pool edge looking like a mythological siren, brazenly watching him die. She watches with a mixture of curiosity and sadness. She weeps.
She pushes the radio into the pool with her foot. It is relaying a cricket match. The last decipherable word is the number 86

(NUMBER 86) before it descends in a distorted burble of sound. She walks around the pool and climbs the steps of the high diving board, pulling her costume back on to her shoulders. She watches him from the top board until he struggles no more, his body floating halfway between the surface and pool bottom. Then, partially etherealized by the bright light shining through all the glass panels, she dives a 'victory' dive.

Section 40: Madgett's Trysting Field

111. EXT. MADGETT'S TRYSTING FIELD. DUSK
From water cut sharply to fire.
A wide shot in the evening. Fingers of orange flame move irregularly across a beige and black striped field. Clouds of orange-white smoke with a low late August sun shining through it.
MADGETT is gorging himself on blackberries picked from the hedge at the side of the field. SMUT is sitting at the side of the field not far from him – eating from a china bowl using a silver spoon to eat his blackberries.
MADGETT and SMUT both have stained fingers, and their chins and shirt fronts are purple with juice – the dye has also stained their cuffs and the brambles have scratched their bare arms, and with SMUT – his bare legs.
Through the yellow smoke and against the burning field, CISSIE 1 and CISSIE 2 come towards them. They are carrying torches.

CISSIE 1: (*Calling out*) Madgett . . . Madgett. What the devil are you doing here?
MADGETT: (*Calmly*) Picking blackberries.
CISSIE 2: We've been looking everywhere for you.
MADGETT: We've been picking blackberries. Vitamin C is good for eunuchs.
CISSIE 2: Eunuchs?
MADGETT: (*Wryly*) Well – I don't use mine . . . and Smut can't use his . . . for the moment.
CISSIE 1: Madgett – are you drunk?
MADGETT: You can't get drunk on blackberries, can you?
CISSIE 2: You smell.
MADGETT: I do – well, I haven't had a bath since Monday.
CISSIE 1: Well, you couldn't say that about Bellamy.

MADGETT: (*With no surprise*) Oh yes? He's been bathing, has he? Maybe drinking it too? Perhaps with a little chlorine in it? More than enough maybe to put out a fire like this?
(*He gestures towards the burning field. In the rapidly gathering dusk, the fires shine brightly – the red illuminating their faces.*)
CISSIE 2: How did you know?
MADGETT: Drownings, like most other things, come in threes.
CISSIE 1: Do they?
CISSIE 2: You're sinister.
MADGETT: (*Laughing, disbelieving*) I'm sinister.
(*Standing with difficulty,* SMUT *empties his pockets, throwing pyrotechnic sparks on to the burning stubble. They crackle and light up red and blue.*)
CISSIE 2: (*Exasperated*) Smut! What's dead now?
SMUT: Everything in this field I would think.
(CISSIE 1 *and* CISSIE 2 *helping* SMUT *– holding his arms – leave the field – silhouettes against the flames and smoke and red and blue squibs.*)

Section 41: *Madgett's Car*

112. INT./EXT. MADGETT'S CAR/COUNTRY ROAD. NIGHT
The two Colpitts women (CISSIE 1 and CISSIE 2) and MADGETT and SMUT drive back in the dark, the two women in the back eating from heaped bowls of blackberries.
MADGETT: How is she?
CISSIE 1: She was crying and shivering when we left.
MADGETT: One of you should have stayed with her.
CISSIE 1: She was wearing a swimsuit.
MADGETT: So? She always wears a swimsuit.
CISSIE 2: She wears one in bed.
MADGETT: Strange girl. Why does she do that, do you think?
CISSIE 2: She's waiting to be called to represent Great Britain in the Olympic Games Women's Relay Team.
The car, in the dark, begins to move among a collection of runners, they are illuminated by the car's headlights – thirty or more silent runners in track shorts, numbered vests and running shoes. It's a hot night, so some of the runners are stripped to their shorts – it may be an illusion, but some of them seem to be running naked. They surround the car, limbs

illuminated by the car headlamps and red rear lamps.
CISSIE 2: Hey – there's Jonah and Moses – Jake's cousins – I didn't know they were keen runners.
CISSIE 1: Good Lord – there's Nancy.
Momentarily in the car lights is a wild and frightened-looking NANCY – hot, sweating and bare-chested. A numbered card is tied around her neck. It is numbered 87 (NUMBER 87).
MADGETT suddenly puts on the brakes. The runners shout and curse, but run on – the car headlamps lighting up their departing backs.
MADGETT: What's all this running for?
CISSIE 2: What have you stopped for?
MADGETT: I've had enough. I'm not helping any more.
CISSIE 1: You must.
MADGETT: Why must I do it?
CISSIE 1: Madgett – you're up to your neck in this.

Section 42: Bellamy's Kitchen

113. INT. BELLAMY'S KITCHEN. NIGHT
Night time in the Bellamy kitchen. BELLAMY lies under a sheet on the apple-green PVC tablecloth on the kitchen table. The neon light flickers erratically in the next room.
The camera set-up is identical to the previous scene in this kitchen. The three CISSIES, MADGETT, and a policeman (the POLICE CORONER) – the same one as present outside the house of the SKIPPING GIRL – are grouped around the table. The POLICE CORONER is writing out a report, which he gets CISSIE 3 to sign – she does so without thinking.
POLICE CORONER: I'm glad you've come, Madgett – I want to discuss something with you. I've got the evidence in the car – excuse me.
(*After a slight pause,* MADGETT *sighs and speaks in a hushed voice.*)
MADGETT: Why have you had Bellamy brought here?
CISSIE 2: She insisted she didn't want him left in the mortuary.
CISSIE 3: Too many strangers – and all of them dead.
MADGETT: So? (MADGETT, *his lower face smeared in purple juice, looks menacing in the flickering neon from the next room.*) Well? It didn't take you long, did it, to drown your husband?

CISSIE 3: Three weeks. (*Offhandedly*) Will they give me bail?
MADGETT: (*Lugubriously*) You only had one husband so you can't drown another – so they might.
CISSIE 3: Do they have swimming pools in prison?
CISSIE 2: Unlikely.
MADGETT: So how come you only gave him three weeks?
CISSIE 3: I was disappointed.
CISSIE 1: I don't really understand what you had to find out that you didn't know before.
CISSIE 3: That was mainly it.
MADGETT: I don't understand why you did it at all.
CISSIE 3: Loyalty, you dope – and I got what I wanted.
MADGETT: Loyalty?
CISSIE 3: I'm going to be sick.
MADGETT: What do you mean, you got what you wanted?
(CISSIE 3 *leans over the sink to vomit and the* POLICE CORONER *returns*.)
POLICE CORONER: Madgett, can I speak here or do you want to come outside?
CISSIE 1: You can speak here.
MADGETT: (*With a smile*) You have your permission. Go ahead.
POLICE CORONER: Well . . . we went to your house looking for you, and we found these. (*He hands over a stack of Polaroids*.) And we discovered some more in a house on Amsterdam Road. (*He hands over some more*.) And, let us say . . . (*He looks at* BELLAMY's *body on the table*) . . . we obtained some from another source. Perhaps you'd like to talk about them?
(MADGETT *peers in exaggerated myopia at the several hundred photographs shuffled in a pack – they show* SMUT *in stages of undress, the cricket photos, the photos of the party on the beach, the photos* SMUT *took of himself flying out of the window*.)
MADGETT: What do you want me to say?
POLICE CORONER: To a casual eye they could be suspicious.
MADGETT: Could they? Cissie – look at these.
(*He hands them around the women*.)
CISSIE 1: It's Smut. His hair has grown a lot in a month, hasn't it?
CISSIE 2: (*Referring to the 'flying' photos*) These are good, aren't they? How did he do it?
POLICE CORONER: And a hospital report?

(*He hands several clipped sheets to* MADGETT – *it's marked with a number 88* (NUMBER 88).)
I believe your son was taken in for what can only be described as sexual mutilation.
(*The women all laugh.*)
CISSIE 2: You'd better ask Smut about that.
POLICE CORONER: You'd better know, Madgett, that you're under investigation.
MADGETT: (*With anxiety*) Whatever for?
POLICE CORONER: For procuring pornography and maybe child abuse?
(*The women all laugh again.* MADGETT *and the women are noticeably relieved.*)
MADGETT: (*Looking at* CISSIE 2) Why don't you throw in a little light necrophilia?
CISSIE 2: You see, Madgett – Smut will get you in the end.
CISSIE 3: (*Breaking in*) We're here to discuss my husband – not the family photographs.
(*After a pause, she pulls back the sheet and looks at* BELLAMY's *naked body in the flickering neon bulb.*)
He could so easily have changed the bulb.
(*On cue, the neon flicks out with a resounding ping. Through the doorway,* SMUT *is balanced on a table, changing the neon strip. The group watches. The new neon is pink.*)
SMUT: This might help.
CISSIE 3: Thank you, Smut.
CISSIE 1: (*Looking at* BELLAMY's *body*) I like his feet.
CISSIE 3: Thank you, Cissie.
CISSIE 2: I like his shoulders.
CISSIE 3: Thank you, Cissie. (*After a pause, and speaking to the* POLICE CORONER) What do you like?
POLICE CORONER: I like a natural death.
MADGETT: Is any death natural?
(*He takes the sheet from* CISSIE 3 *and re-covers the body.*)
CISSIE 3: (*After a pause*) I liked his bollocks. (*She sadly and gently places her hand on his genitals masked by the sheet. Then she says brightly:*) Are widows eligible for the Olympic Games?

Section 43: The Walnut Tree

114. EXT. MADGETT'S HOUSE – GARDEN. DAY

The walnut tree at the end of Madgett's garden that overlooks the river. A warm, early autumn day.
In the topmost branches of the walnut tree, SMUT, wearing a T-shirt and short trousers, red socks and plimsolls, with a canvas bag around his shoulder tied to his waist with a string, holds a can of yellow paint. With some delicacy and concern for the leaves, he methodically works down the branches putting a small but noticeable spot of yellow paint on the top side of each leaf. He counts as he spot-paints. When he gets to the end of each branch, he binds it at its lowest point with a length of bright red raffia, and in a notebook kept in the canvas bag, he keeps a tally with a chewed red pencil. He is totally absorbed in this activity, counting silently in the tens of thousands mark.
The camera watches SMUT, then slowly moves down and among the leaves of the mature tree to reveal MADGETT reclining on a sagging hammock, his feet bare, his eyes peeping out from under a book that shades his head from the sun. CISSIE 1 sits in an armchair shelling peas into a metal colander that glints in the sun. CISSIE 2 sits in a deckchair. CISSIE 3 lies on a blanket on the grass. MADGETT watches the women from under the book

that shades his head – watching with some delight and some lechery. They are surrounded by sheep.

CISSIE 3: What on earth do you keep all those sheep for?
MADGETT: I like sheep – don't you like sheep?
CISSIE 3: (*Uncertain*) Yes.
MADGETT: I keep them for emergencies.
CISSIE 2: What emergencies?
MADGETT: Sleepless nights. I count best at night.
CISSIE 2: (*Looking up*) We all count best at night.
(*Yellow sticky paint drops from on high. It falls, splashing in a circle at* CISSIE 3*'s feet.*)
CISSIE 3: That's it, Smut – not an inch further or I'll shake you out of that tree.
CISSIE 1: (*Looking up*) What's he doing?
MADGETT: Counting the leaves.
CISSIE 2: Whatever for?
MADGETT: Haven't you ever wondered how many leaves there were on a tree?
CISSIE 2: Never.
MADGETT: Or hairs on your head?
CISSIES 2 and 3: (*Together*) No.
MADGETT: Or fish in the sea?
CISSIES 1, 2 and 3: (*Together*) No.
CISSIE 1: On Saturday, we'll put the ashes in the sea – or rather the river. You, Madgett, can be our witness.
MADGETT: What do you want a witness for?
CISSIE 1: To make sure we do it correctly, of course.
MADGETT: Isn't it illegal?
SMUT: (*Shouting down from the tree*) NO!
(MADGETT *and the three* CISSIES *look up.*)

Section 44: Crematorium 3

115. EXT. CREMATORIUM 3 AND WATER TOWER 3. DAY
A crematorium garden. Overshadowing or overlooking the garden and the gravestones is a gaunt water tower. There are bells. The three Colpitts women stand in a line in their funeral clothes. The 'water tower' conspirators are grouped together and framed, under the water tower.

CISSIE 1: (*Looking around at the tower and at the conspirators*) Well . . . we're all together here – no need for secrecy.

CISSIE 2: (*To* CISSIE 3) What on earth made you choose this place?
CISSIE 3: I thought the tower would mean we could keep them all under surveillance.
(*A wide shot reveals graves marked with 89 and 90, a garden plot marked 91.* (NUMBERS 89, 90 and 91).)
CISSIE 1: Who officially invited them?
CISSIE 3: They invited themselves.
CISSIE 1: Are you sure Madgett didn't say something? They look like an old-fashioned band of mourners.
CISSIE 2: And there's the pyrotechnical expert.
(*The three women walk a few paces to where* SMUT *is crouched over some rockets propped up in milk bottles. He is trying and failing to set them alight.*)
SMUT: They just won't light. They're too damp – it's not surprising. (*Throwing away a match in disgust*) Bellamy was pretty wet – even out of water.

Section 45: Madgett's Car

116. INT./EXT. MADGETT'S CAR/ROAD/BEACH. DAY
The return from the cemetery – the women in their funeral clothes are sitting in the back of Madgett's car. SMUT and MADGETT are in front. All are engrossed. It's a windy day. The sea is very close, though not visible from the car.
MADGETT: Stop! Can you smell that?
MADGETT stops the car. Silence. Sound of the wind. He gets half out of the car. One foot on the road, the breeze blows his hair and his tie. He sniffs, closes door and drives sharply to the left, down a sandy track between dunes to the beach. MADGETT and SMUT get out, SMUT taking his pot of paint and some stakes. The three women sit still in the back of the car.
CISSIE 2: Where's he gone now?

117. EXT. DEAD FISH BEACH. DAY
The women get out and walk the few yards to the top of a dune, and look down on the beach.
The beach is crowded with dead fish. The sea has thrown up a shoal – mostly herring. Some are still alive, some dying, most dead. SMUT has already staked out sections, marked the stakes with red paint and is counting the fish. MADGETT is throwing

live ones back in. There are thousands of gulls.
On the dunetop, the Colpitts women look down.
   CISSIE 3: That man has a nose for a corpse.
   CISSIE 2: His son is quicker.
   CISSIE 1: What *are* they – some sort of carrion?
   (*There is a pause as they walk slowly towards* MADGETT *and* SMUT *who are engrossed among the dead fish that sparkle and shine in the sunlight.*)
   CISSIE 2: (*To* CISSIE 3) You know you've got yours coming to you . . . ?
   CISSIE 3: What?
   CISSIE 1: An invitation to that field near Brough . . .
   CISSIE 2: . . . that is surrounded by that thick hedge . . .
   CISSIE 1: . . . where Smut is sent to catch moths and never returns with any.
   CISSIE 2: Madgett's harmless. With that large carcass and all that bluff conversation . . . and that mania for eating.
   CISSIE 1: (*Quietly, after a pause and aiming to be provocative*) I wouldn't mind.
   CISSIE 3: What wouldn't you mind?
   CISSIE 2: It would be like sleeping with your uncle.
   CISSIE 1: It would be like bribing the referee.
   CISSIE 3: What would?
   CISSIE 2: He's more than a referee. Poor Madgett! It's like the story of Billy Goat Gruff!
   CISSIE 3: What is?
   CISSIE 1: With Madgett as the Goblin under the bridge.
   CISSIE 2: Do you really think the grass is greener across the stream?
   CISSIE 1: Without a doubt. (*She turns over a dead fish with her foot.*) Hey! These are herring – do you think they're edible?
   CISSIE 2: Now, Cissie, it's your turn.
   (*She looks at* CISSIE 3.)
   CISSIE 3: I like his hands – I might let him touch me and then I could tell you all about it.
   CISSIE 1: Well, you're the last in the line.
   CISSIE 3: What if he was to be disappointed?
   CISSIE 2: That might spoil it. (*With a giggle*) You better not go too far then.
   CISSIE 3: If one of us made it with him, it would surely exclude the other two.
   (*They laugh.*)

CISSIE 1: I doubt if Madgett could get it up three times in an afternoon.
(CISSIE 2 *and* CISSIE 3 *both exclaim together* 'Cissie!' *They are almost up to* MADGETT. SMUT *is further off chasing gulls.*)
CISSIE 2: Madgett, we've been talking about you.
MADGETT: I know.
CISSIE 1: Could you get it up three times in an afternoon?
(CISSIE 1 *and* CISSIE 2 *each take* MADGETT's *arm – one on the right, one on the left.* MADGETT *blushes deeply.*)
MADGETT: (*Looking away to the sea, and speaking very quietly*) I'd like to try. It depends who's asking me.
CISSIE 3: Hey – look at this. These fish are all numbered – look.
(*The Colpitts women are amazed, for all the fish have small, red plastic tags affixed to them. We can see numbers 92, 93 and 94* (NUMBERS 92, 93 *and* 94). *It is a wonder that the numbers have not been seen before.*)
CISSIE 2: Smut! Did you organize this?
(*From a distance he smiles enigmatically, but doesn't answer.*)

Section 46: *Madgett's Trysting Field*

118. INT./EXT. MADGETT'S CAR/TRYSTING FIELD. NIGHT
The black car is isolated in the middle of a field under a starry sky. It's surrounded by standing and sitting sheep, all chewing the cud. The sound of a distant cock pheasant.
Medium shot of the car showing CISSIE 3 and MADGETT sitting in the front seat of the car under the orange light. They are deep in conversation. The skull-like, blank faces of the sheep surround the bodywork of the car.
Close-up of CISSIE 3 and MADGETT sitting in the car.

   CISSIE 3: Madgett . . . are you now going to try the same thing on me as you tried on the others . . . ?
   (MADGETT *doesn't reply*.)
You don't think Bellamy drowned to make way for you, do you?
   MADGETT: It's strange.
   (*He stares wistfully and absently into the dark field*.)
   CISSIE 3: What is?
   MADGETT: How this field is synonymous with my failure.
   CISSIE 3: It's a beautiful place – where's Smut?
   MADGETT: He wouldn't come any more.
   CISSIE 3: I don't blame him.
   MADGETT: Three rebuffs in the same place. That must be a record.
   CISSIE 3: (*Laughing*) Sounds to me you should have more imagination.
   (MADGETT *doesn't answer*.)
You can't swim . . . can you, Madgett?
   (*He looks at her*.)
Anyway I'm too young for you. I suppose you're in a good position to try blackmail. You could put all three of us away if you wanted to.
   MADGETT: That's the last thing I want to do.
   CISSIE 3: I believe you. (*She smiles*.) Since you've had such bad luck with the others – I'll let you go a little of the way.
   MADGETT: (*Smiling sadly*) As compensation?
   (CISSIE 3 *unbuttons her dress – she is wearing her ubiquitous swimsuit underneath her dress – it leaves little to the imagination*.

She takes MADGETT's *hand and puts it on her breast.*)
CISSIE 3: Put your hand here.
(MADGETT, *surprised, does as he's told.*)
I've watched you watching me. I've watched you watching us all. Do you think we're the same woman?
(MADGETT *slides his hand inside her costume – she doesn't resist.*)
MADGETT: Sometimes I do.
CISSIE 3: Just because we've got the same name.
MADGETT: No.
CISSIE 3: Why then?
MADGETT: Because of your camaraderie.
CISSIE 3: Our what?
MADGETT: Your friendship for one another.
CISSIE 3: You know that I'm pregnant?
MADGETT: Was three weeks enough?
(*He slides her costume from her shoulders.*)
CISSIE 3: Madgett, don't be so innocent. Three weeks was long enough to legitimize. You can kiss me here.
(*She indicates her nipple.*)
MADGETT: Will I taste anything?
CISSIE 3: (*Laughing*) Not yet, you dope.
MADGETT: (*Indicating her costume*) Take the rest off.
CISSIE 3: No, Madgett – I'm a widow of forty-eight hours.
MADGETT: So?
(MADGETT *begins to make strenuous moves to undress* CISSIE 3. *They begin to struggle in the cramped space at the front of the car – the small orange light revealing the shadowy action. The windows begin to steam up by degrees.*)
CISSIE 3: Madgett – that's enough! (*Half coquettishly*) You must be satisfied with small services – a little at a time.
MADGETT: Must I? Is saving you from prison a small service?
CISSIE 3: It was death through misadventure.
MADGETT: Was it? Quite a few people don't see it that way at all.
CISSIE 3: To hell with the others.
MADGETT: You're deliberately provoking me.
CISSIE 3: (*Provokingly*) Am I?
(MADGETT *tries to kiss her and fumbles again at her costume.*)
Madgett – thank you for making me see reason.
MADGETT: Reason? About what?
CISSIE 3: About Bellamy.
MADGETT: I didn't do that – it was Cissie.

CISSIE 3: Well, you made it possible.
MADGETT: I did?
CISSIE 3: Of course. I knew that when I married Bellamy, with you around, when the time came, I could drown him.
MADGETT: You what!
(*With mingled anger and frustration*, MADGETT *pulls off the top half of* CISSIE 3*'s swimming costume*.)
CISSIE 3: (*Still very self-possessed*) Madgett – is this attempted rape?
MADGETT: You Colpitts women have used me.
CISSIE 3: Madgett! You're supposed to be harmless – pack it in.
(*They struggle vigorously*.)
MADGETT: You women have destroyed me!
CISSIE 3: Don't be so melodramatic!

119. EXT. MADGETT'S TRYSTING FIELD. DAY
As seen from a medium shot outside in the field – the sheep grouped around the car – the car windows partly steamed up and lit from inside with the orange light – the shadows of violent movement seen inside.
Suddenly the front nearside door flies open and CISSIE 3, half leaping, half falling, dishevelled and half undressed, sprawls on the grass.
A top shot reveals the car with the sheep dramatically exploding in escape from the car's vicinity – running to all sides of the dark field. CISSIE 3 runs off holding her head which is bleeding just below the hairline.

Section 47: *The Skipping Girl's House*

120. INT./EXT. SKIPPING GIRL'S HOUSE. NIGHT
The light from the corridor of the GIRL's house is warm and orange. SMUT, with his notebook, sits on the girl's chair just inside the door. The GIRL, more elaborately dressed than ever before, skips very confidently on the pavement. Sometimes she – daringly – skips almost on the kerb edge.
  SMUT: The best days for violent deaths are Wednesdays – red-letter days – so much so that I keep running out of red paint.

Saturday (*He consults his notebook.*) is second best – in the afternoon. Tuesday is the third best – or worst. The safest time of all is Friday night – tonight, in fact – between teatime and midnight. (*He looks up at the* GIRL.) Are you going to a party tonight?
(*The* HARE *in the paper chase runs down the street scattering papers in the street lights. The children give him a casual glance.*)
GIRL: (*Without stopping*) Yes. On a boat. We're to have pineapple fruit salad, cheese with walnuts. And I'm going to dance.
SMUT: What size shoe do you take?
GIRL: 34 – Continental size.
SMUT: The river is full of shoes. I'll find you some that fit. (*He studies her, gets up, looks up and down the road. Very matter-of-fact*) Elsie? I love you, will you give me a kiss?
GIRL: All right – just here.
(*She points to her cheek.* SMUT *tries to kiss her cheek, but she refuses to stop skipping.*)
SMUT: I've done what you asked me to do.
GIRL: What's that?
SMUT: Circumcised myself – do you want to look?
GIRL: (*Unabashed*) No, thank you – not today.
Just then, Madgett's car pulls up alongside the kerb. MADGETT leans over and opens the nearside door for SMUT. SMUT picks up his notebook from the step and gets in. The car moves off.
SMUT: You've scratched your cheek.
MADGETT: I know.
SMUT turns around in his seat to wave to the SKIPPING GIRL. She moves tentatively into the road after MADGETT's car has gone. With confidence she begins to skip with renewed skill while she looks up at the stars. She starts to count them.
GIRL: One . . . Alpha Centauri . . . Two . . . Canopus . . . Three . . . Polydeuces . . . Four . . . Agamemnon . . . Five . . . Pegasus Delta . . .
A second car – jammed with the road-runners, pursuers in the paperchase – comes rapidly down the road following the trail of papers down the kerb. The car is packed with sweaty bodies. Their numbered vests press against the windows – numbers 95 and 96 (NUMBERS 95 and 96) are very visible. NANCY is visible in the back seat and JONAH BOGNOR is driving. The car runs down the SKIPPING GIRL and leaves her dead in the road. Her hand still clutches both handles of the skipping rope.

Section 48: Madgett's House

121. EXT. MADGETT'S HOUSE – BEACH. DAY
Endgame. On the foreshore outside Madgett's house. It's a fresher, more blustery morning than other mornings.
A wide shot reveals the beach. MADGETT, dressed in his ill-fitting funeral suit, sits on a battered chair – one of several previously used in earlier beach games – the dummy seen before is seated on one of the chairs. MADGETT and the chairs are hemmed in with sheep whose bodies hide the beach floor. MADGETT is dolefully eating chocolate pudding from a large bowl.
SMUT, GREGORY and SID THE DIGGER are also on the beach. SID sits on the low beach wall polishing his spade with an oily rag, SMUT and GREGORY are hoisting a storm-warning sign on the flagpole. On the waterline is a rowing boat.

122. EXT. MADGETT'S HOUSE – BEACH. DAY
At the top of the beach, a local taxi pulls up and the three CISSIE COLPITTS get out and prepare to come down the beach. CISSIE 2 calls to SMUT, who is forever hitching up his oversize trousers – the short trousers of his dark suit – to come and collect two cardboard grocery boxes taken out of the taxi. GREGORY goes with SMUT. They take the boxes down to the rowboat.

123. EXT. MADGETT'S HOUSE – BEACH. DAY
The Colpitts women come down on to the beach, the sheep moving out of their way. The taxi's registration number is JYT 97 (NUMBER 97).
  CISSIE 1: Good morning, Madgett, what's the game today?
  MADGETT: (*Without looking up and avoiding the women's eyes*) Tug-of-war.
  CISSIE 2: Ah. In honour of the dead? How symbolic. Life versus death?
  (*The sheep have moved away sufficiently to reveal a heavy rope laid out on the beach. It is tied with coloured rags at intervals.*)
  CISSIE 3: Good morning, Madgett – I hope you've recovered. Don't look so miserable. (*She kisses him on the forehead.*) You were sorely provoked. What can I do about my eye?

(*Her eye is bruised from the previous evening's happenings.*)
MADGETT: Get Smut to give you some sheep's liver.
CISSIE 1: (*Laughing*) Rubbish, Madgett. (*Indicating the rope with her foot*) Who is going to play this game?
MADGETT: Good and evil.
CISSIE 2: Who's good and who's evil?
MADGETT: Depends on how you look at it.
CISSIE 3: What are they playing for?
MADGETT: Me, and what's left of my reputation.
CISSIE 2: (*Laughing affectionately*) As a man or as a coroner?
MADGETT: (*Very quietly*) Both. If they win I give in . . .
CISSIE 1: If who wins?

124. EXT. MADGETT'S HOUSE – BEACH. DAY
As if in answer to the question, a car draws up on the foreshore road and out get the water-tower conspirators – NANCY, JAKE's cousins, MRS HARDY, BELLAMY'S SISTER, the two runners from the beach. The car's registration number is DYB 98 (NUMBER 98).

125. EXT. MADGETT'S HOUSE – BEACH. DAY
CISSIE 2: God, Madgett – did you invite them?
MADGETT: (*With a wan smile*) No.
CISSIE 1: They have a nose for a funeral.
CISSIE 3: There are seven of them.
MADGETT: Then we can't complain.
CISSIE 1: Madgett – what are you up to?
MADGETT: Well – they ought to be here, didn't they? You don't want to be accused of secret burials, do you . . . ? And since there are obviously no rewards for me helping you, I thought enough was enough; I'm having trouble remembering which death I'm writing certificates for and so I'm considering setting the records straight. I've arranged to let the outcome hang on a game of wit and strength.
(*He smiles, amused at their obvious concern.*)
CISSIE 3: Come on, Madgett – you'll never get them to play.
MADGETT: If the stakes are high enough, they will.
(*The water-tower conspirators begin to come down on to the beach.*)
CISSIE 1: Physically they're stronger than us.
MADGETT: Morally as well I would have thought.
CISSIE 2: (*Getting really concerned*) Madgett – I do believe you're serious.

CISSIE 3: Madgett, we're not letting you go that easily.
MADGETT: Letting me go? If I go, you go too. That's the stakes – if we lose, we all go.
CISSIE 1: Madgett, we were not party to this – your game-playing is your affair.
MADGETT: I've had enough game-playing – this is for real. Besides, you're much better at playing games than I am.
CISSIE 2: This game is very dangerous.
MADGETT: God – haven't I told you – all games are dangerous.
(*The water-tower conspirators have come within earshot.*)
JONAH: What games? I thought we were burying ashes. (*Sarcastically, looking at* SID THE DIGGER) I see you've got the gravedigger with you.
CISSIE 3: Sid's going to row the boat – that's all – the ashes are going on the river.
MRS HARDY: A nice provocative gesture.
CISSIE 1: Not at all, Mrs Hardy.
MRS HARDY: No son of mine would want to be cremated and then thrown in the water.
CISSIE 2: Then that's where you're wrong. Hardy had a fear of burial second only to his fear of growing thin through starvation.
MADGETT: (*Interrupting the growing provocation*) We thought as a fitting send-off, we'd play a game.
The HARE *from the paperchase approaches with the linen bag over his shoulder. His bag is nearly empty. He throws the last paper – thin shreds of red tissue on to the sand, and stands and watches.*
MOSES: A game!
JONAH: What sort of game?
NANCY: Watch him – he's always playing games.
JONAH: (*Insidiously*) Don't worry, Nancy, we'll look after you.
GREGORY: You watch what you're saying to my sister.
RUNNER 70: Let's do as he says.
MARINA: This is no time to be playing games.
MRS HARDY: He's like a kid.
SMUT: (*Picking up the rope*) It's just a tug-of-war.
MRS HARDY: And that boy of yours, Madgett – he's got a thing or two to tell.
MADGETT: We feel we owe you an explanation.
CISSIE 3: Shut up, Madgett.

JONAH: An explanation? You owe us more than a bloody explanation.
MOSES: All right, we'll play your game – we'll beat you easily and then wrap the rope around your neck, Madgett.
MARINA: And then you'll come with us.
CISSIE 2: If you win.
MARINA: Win?
CISSIE 2: Win the game.
RUNNER 71: What's it got to do with winning?
MADGETT: Those are the stakes – you win and you'll get your explanation.

126. EXT. MADGETT'S HOUSE – BEACH. DAY
The runner from the paperchase throws his empty bag into the rowboat. Having got themselves into an antagonistic state, both sides pick up the rope, jostle for a position, and on a signal from the runner – the HARE from the paperchase – they start to pull. The tug-of-war on the beach (with a storm gathering behind and the sheep bleating) has attracted several onlookers. Far down the beach comes a party of runners – the same runners we've seen before.
The two teams are equally matched and little ground has been lost by either team, when a police car, its blue lamp flashing, pulls up on the beach road.

Tug-of-War

> SMUT: (*Voice over*) The game of Tug-of-war is played with as many people as there is room for along the rope. The sides need to be evenly matched with weight and strength to make it an interesting contest. At an agreed signal, each team tries to pull the other over an agreed mark or space previously decided on. Seven a side is an ideal number of players for tug-of-war . . . for seven is the number of the days of the week, the colours of the rainbow, the seven seas, the primary planets, the seven dwarfs, the deadly sins, the ages of man and the wonders of the world.

The competitors, without relaxing an inch, all look towards the police car with curiosity and some apprehension. A POLICEMAN gets out of the car, comes to the edge of the beach and calls out SMUT's name. SMUT, for a moment, just looks.

The POLICEMAN beckons and SMUT lets go of his hold on the rope. The evenly matched teams are suddenly released from their tension. The water-tower conspirators fall backwards, the MADGETT team is pulled across the line. SMUT walks up the beach and doesn't look back. There are screams from the Colpitts women.

> CISSIE 1: Smut! Smut! You've let us down, Smut!
> CISSIE 2: (*Getting up and throwing down the rope*) Come on, quick, get in the boat.
> JONAH: We've won. Time to call it a day, Madgett.
> CISSIE 3: Sid, Gregory, we've got to get Madgett in the boat. Come on.
> MADGETT: It's no use, Cissie, the police are here.
> CISSIE 2: (*Sarcastically*) They've come to see Smut, not us . . . they can't touch him.

The distant runners have arrived abreast of the activity – for a moment their presence distracts the attention and impetus of the water-tower conspirators. The runners are dressed in cover-all see-through plastic bags – maybe they are anticipating rain. The distraction is enough to give the CISSIES, with SID's and GREGORY's help, enough time to reach the boat with the somnambulant MADGETT.

127. EXT. MADGETT'S HOUSE – BEACH. DAY
SMUT approaches the POLICEMAN who tells him something – something unheard. He hands him a bunch of skipping ropes – eight of them, all variously coloured. SMUT takes them and slowly puts them around his neck. He looks shaken, goes to the beach edge and waves down at the CISSIES and MADGETT in the boat; they are too busy getting the boat afloat to wave back – or notice him. SMUT walks up to Madgett's house.

128. EXT. MADGETT'S HOUSE – WATER'S EDGE. DAY
On the water's edge, CISSIES 2 and 3 and GREGORY are pushing the boat out into the choppy water. The CISSIES are wet to the waist. MADGETT sits blankly in the boat. The water-tower conspirators come down the beach. SID strides up the beach between them, carrying his spade with some menace. They part to let him through. The women get into the boat, CISSIE 3 holding up the casket of BELLAMY's ashes to the crowd on the beach.
    CISSIE 3: Do you want to say a few last words?
    JONAH: There'll be plenty to say when you get back.
The boat pulls away from the shore – CISSIE 2 at the oars. The water-tower conspirators turn with some expectation to the police car – but it's leaving.
    CISSIE 1: There's a storm coming, Madgett.
    CISSIE 2: Can you swim?
    MADGETT: (*Lugubriously*) No.
    CISSIE 3: I thought not.
    CISSIE 1: (*Putting her arm round* MADGETT's *shoulders*) Dear me, Madgett, lechery, gluttony *and* you can't swim – you seem to have all the nicest and most convenient vices rolled into one. Never mind. You can read the burial service.
(*The Colpitts women look excited – like triumphant sirens.*)

129. EXT. MADGETT'S HOUSE – GARDEN. DAY

SMUT walks straight up to the walnut tree in Madgett's garden. The skipping ropes are still around his neck. He collects the yellow paint pot, the brush and his notebook from the bottom of the ladder and climbs up into the tree. His dog – still with the curling papers attached to its fur – stops and sits at the base of the tree.

As SMUT disappears into the lower branches, SID THE DIGGER appears with his shiny spade. He waits at a distance, lighting a cigarette.

Up in the tree, SMUT carefully ties a skipping rope to a branch and makes a noose which he puts over his neck. Then with some assumed nonchalance, he starts to count the leaves of the tree, marking each one with a spot of yellow paint. The distant storm clouds can be seen through the trees. SMUT, half experimentally, half accidentally, tries slipping his foot off the branch he's standing on.

In mockery of all the other games to which he has added his voice as reader of the rules, SMUT now makes up rules for the game he is about to play.

The Endgame

> SMUT: (*Voice over*) The object of this game is to dare to fall with a noose around your neck from a place sufficiently off the ground such that a fall will hang you. The object of the game is to punish those who have caused great unhappiness by their selfish actions. This is the best game of all because the winner is also the loser and the judge's decision is always final.

SMUT's foot slips, and in a flurry of leaves, he falls. His head

lodges in the Y-fork of two branches. The skipping rope is still slack. His neck is broken from a fall that didn't involve the skipping rope. The yellow paint dribbles down his arm and down his leg and drops on to the grass – like custard. The pencil attached to the pad hangs and swings in the breeze – its last entry is the number 99 (NUMBER 99).
SID THE DIGGER sticks his spade into the ground, walks over to the hanging figure of SMUT and hitches up the boy's trousers. He goes over to some bushes, and, with the cigarette from his mouth, he ignites a fuse hidden among the leaves. He then returns to the foot of the tree, adroitly marks out a hole and begins to dig. A grave.
A large and spectacular rocket is launched not far from the walnut tree. SID doesn't look round. Five seconds later and a few feet further away a second rocket rushes up into the sky. Then a third.

130. EXT. MADGETT'S HOUSE – SEA. DAY
In the boat on the choppy water. The fireworks can be seen on the mainland, shooting up against the storm clouds.
 CISSIE 1: What on earth is Smut celebrating – we lost.
 MADGETT: He arranged a spectacle for the scattering of the ashes.
 CISSIE 2: Thoughtful boy.

CISSIE 3: Well, Madgett, how do you feel about things now?
MADGETT: No different – as I said – we lost. I've had enough.
CISSIE 3: Well, Madgett, we haven't lost and there is no question of any of us giving in.
MADGETT: What are you going to do?

CISSIE 3 *begins to take off her dress – she has a swimming costume on underneath.* MADGETT *thinks nothing of it because* CISSIE 3 *always has a swimming costume on.*

CISSIE 3: There's a storm coming up. I thought I'd be prepared.
CISSIE 2: Are you going to undress too, Madgett? That way we could make it look like a proper accident.
CISSIE 3: Come on, Madgett – off with your clothes – it'll make it a neater ending . . . what an opportunity alone in an open boat with the women you love and an invitation to undress.
CISSIE 2: (*Quietly*) Don't worry about Smut. He'll be all right.

MADGETT, *with a fatalistic gesture, begins to pull off his tie. It pulls at once into a knot.* CISSIE 2 *helps him out of it.* CISSIE 3 *has rowed the boat more or less into the centre of the river.*

CISSIE 1: (*As* MADGETT *begins to take off his jacket*) Wait a minute – let's keep it a little dignified – first the burial service.

CISSIE 2 takes a wooden mallet and a chisel and begins to knock out the bung at the bottom of the boat. CISSIE 1 takes out JAKE's battered, half-burned fork and, holding it momentarily over the side, lets it slip into the water. It disappears at once.

CISSIE 1: In loving memory of a Gardener.

CISSIE 3 helps CISSIE 2 lift out the heavy sand-clogged typewriter and together they hold it over the side of the boat. They drop it in and retreat back from the splash.

CISSIE 2: In loving memory of a Businessman.

CISSIE 3 takes out the damp radio that belonged to BELLAMY. She turns it on and tunes it – coming across a local radio weather forecast that announces bad weather and a storm on the river. Laughing, the three CISSIES watch as CISSIE 3 holds it momentarily above the water and then lets it drop. It doesn't sink at once; buoyed up by an inner air pocket, it floats before sinking with a slow gurgle and a distortion in the announcer's voice.

CISSIE 3: In loving memory of . . . an . . . unemployed . . . Non-Swimmer . . .

In spite of their mocking behaviour, all three women are somewhat disturbed. MADGETT sits watching them – slowly taking off his shoes and socks.

Quietly, without saying a word, CISSIE 1 takes the casket of JAKE's ashes and drops them gently over the side, throwing red flowers after it. The other two CISSIES do likewise. MADGETT slowly takes off his shirt. The remainder of the red flowers in the grocery box are thrown in the water. They are the same colour and species as were illustrated on the calendar that announced the start of the series of numbers. CISSIE 1 sighs, gets up and kisses the quiet, sad-faced MADGETT on the mouth, brushing his face and body with her hair. With greater intimacy, CISSIE 2 does likewise, CISSIE 3 kisses him the hardest, hugging his face to her breasts.

131. EXT. MADGETT'S HOUSE – SEA. DAY
The water in the boat is now rising fast. The women jump off the side of the boat and, laughing, swim away through the red floating flowers. MADGETT takes off his trousers and his pants and his wristwatch – he puts them in the grocery box which is now afloat.
The fireworks still shoot up on the mainland as, for the first time, a framing of the rowboat clearly shows that it has the number 100 painted on its prow (NUMBER 100).

132. EXT. MADGETT'S HOUSE – SEA. DAY
Stripped to drown, much like the corpses he pronounced on, MADGETT resignedly waits for the boat to sink.

The Number Count

For those who may be curious, and for those who doubt that all the numbers in the number-count from **1** to **100** finally made it into the film, here is a full list. There are other possible lists.

Number **1** appears in the first scene after the main title – boldly white on a tree that was set upright after the ravages of the October 1987 hurricane. **2** appears on a tin bath holding windfall apples that Nancy drunkenly tips out on to the grass in the moonlit garden. **3** is a laundry mark on Jake's discarded blue-and-white striped shirt. **4** and **5** are in the text – Four-in-hand and Five-card-stud – games that, according to the drunken Jake, Madgett is supposed to play with Cissie 1. **6** is beside Madgett's telephone in his bedroom; **7** is the seven-of-hearts playing-cards that make up Smut's castle. **8** and **9** are in Hardy's bedroom – **8** on a digital alarm-clock, **9** on a key-ring.

10 is the end of Smut's number count as he prepares to jump from his bedroom window. **11** and **12** number the Polaroids of Smut jumping. **13** is painted in white on the pitch-blacked barn wall; **14** is beside the telephone and **15** is a number on a cricket pad – both in Madgett's bedroom. **16** is on the wheelbarrow carrying the comatose Nancy home to bed. **17** is the first evidence seen of Smut's clerical necrophilia – to mark the site of the dead cockerel which needed to crow three times before the phone could be answered. **18**, **19** and **20** are on Nancy's rabbit-hutches.

21 is the number on Nancy's yellow front door. **22** is *Catch 22* – Nancy's bedside reading; **23** is how old Nancy is – a birthday card is propped up in her room full of rabbits and shoes. **24**, **25**, **26**, **27** and **28** are part of Smut's ambitious counting of the hairs of a dog. **29** is the corpse-ticket in Smut's matchbox. **30** is the number of matches in the box, **31** is tied to the celebratory firework. **32** is the number painted on the road among the flies to mark the bloodied and unrecognizable corpse. **33** is on Smut's stake to mark the site of the death of Jake and **34** is in the text – the number of years Cissie 1 reckons she's lived with Jake. **35** is the number of a star – Groombridge 35 – that Smut has found for the Skipping Girl. **36** is in red on the green swimsuit of Cissie 3 as she leaves the river. **37**, **38** and **39** are numbered insects in Smut's entomological textbook featuring the Elephant Hawk Moth.

Dominoes in Madgett's bedroom make the figure **40**. **41** is the location of an unburied corpse supplied by Smut to Sid, the gravedigger. **42** is stencilled on a bee-hive. **43** is on Cissie 3's bathing cap in the swimming-pool and **44** is the combination of two numbers in a changing cubicle. **45** and **46** are numbered bees. **47** is on the foreground wooden stake in the churchyard memorial service of Jake; **48** is one of the numbers counted in threes by the Colpitts women as they try to mask out the priest's burial service. **49** is a large white number on the conspirator's water-tower and **50** is a large, yellow marker at Bellamy's wedding party on the beach at Cissie 2's house.

51 is in the text – the number of runs made by the batsman Chapman Ridger. **52** is the summer of 1952 when the batsman Hollinghurst was fatally struck on the top of the head at Headingley. **53** is a black number on the side of a canvas tent. **54** is another of Smut's notifications to Sid the gravedigger of an unburied corpse. **55** numbers a Polaroid of Nancy. **56** to **60** come in a flurry in Madgett's bedroom – **56** is on a left-handed bat, **57** on the back of the camera Madgett uses to take photographs of Smut. **58** is in the text – the number of runs made by the batsman Tolley Schriker before he fell down the pavilion steps. **59** is on the white spot of a bowls ball.

60 is the mark of a cricketing tragedy on Smut's naked shoulder. **61**, **62** and **63** are numbers in Smut's torch-illuminated entomological textbook. **64** is a number on the back of the night-time runner throwing paper streamers into the headlamps of Madgett's car. **65** and **66** are in Hardy's typewritten letter to his insurance company complaining of a robbery at the firework factory. **67**, **68** and **69** are numbers that Cissie 2 experimentally types on her husband's lemonade-soaked typewriter.

Mr **70** and Mr **71** Van Dyke are runners in the paperchase – potential witnesses to Hardy's murder. **72** is in the text and refers to the page number in the *Book of Common Prayer* at Hardy's funeral service. **73** is a number on a pew in the Wesleyan chapel where Hardy's commemorative service is held. **74** is the hymn number propped up on the modest chapel organ. **75** is in the text – the ideal number of players in a game of Hangman's Cricket – six sides of 12 and three umpires. **76** and **77** are numbers on the rumps of live cows. **78** and **79** are numbers on the rumps of dead cows.

80, **81** and **82** are figures in an entomological textbook Smut abandons to circumcise himself. **83** is the freak reflection on Smut's bedroom window. **84** is a silvered stencil hanging on his wall. **85** is the number on the key-ring hanging around Cissie 3's neck when she drowns Bellamy. **86** is the last decipherable score in an unidentified cricket match heard on Bellamy's drowning radio. **87** is the number around Nancy's neck as she runs with the Bognor Brothers through the burning stubble.

88, **89** and **90** are numbers in Bellamy's seaside squat – a room at the end of the pier. **88** is on a motorbike, **89** is on the back of the detective's clipboard and **90** is hung above the bar that has been converted into a kitchen.

91 is boldly hung on Smut's tree beside the estuary. **92**, **93** and **94** are ticketed dead herring. **95** is on the numbered vest of the hare as he runs in front of the Skipping Girl, a few minutes before her death. **96** is on the numbered vest of a runner among the pack following the paper-chase to Madgett's jetty. **97** is on the taxi that brought the Colpitts women to the tug-of-war and **98** is on the car that brought the conspirators.

99 is Smut's last recorded writing, in the notebook that hangs around his neck – evidence of his contribution and knowledge of the number count. Perhaps, after all, it was he who engineered the whole business. And **100** is painted on the prow of Madgett's rowing-boat – the instrument of his apparent drowning, and the last image of the film. When your number comes around . . . The count is complete and the film is finished.